A pulse-racing ne...

Sexy Surgeons in the City

Bachelor brothers in the Big Apple!

To the outside world, siblings and surgeons
Logan and Sam Grant have it all. Born into a vastly
wealthy family and with staggeringly successful
medical careers of their own, they have Manhattan
at their feet. Or do they...?

Their relationships with their family are strained, and
when it comes to finding *the one*, it seems their luck
has truly run out. So for now they're focusing on their
ever-deserving patients and their first love—medicine.
It would take two very special women for the brothers
to allow themselves to be swept up into a whirlwind of
romance again...and they may just have found them!

Logan let ex-wife Harper slip through his fingers
once. He can only wonder if it's fate that's brought
her through the doors of his hospital... Can he win her
back? And does she want to be won...?

Find out in

Manhattan Marriage Reunion by JC Harroway

Burned by love, Sam is plowing his passion
into his work, until his new colleague Lucy charms
her way into his guarded heart in

New York Nights with Mr. Right by Tina Beckett

Both available now!

Dear Reader,

Writing this second-chance romance allowed me to imagine the emotional journey of two people who'd been deeply in love before, messed up and then reunited years later. All of the things they like about each other are still there: the familiarity, the memories, the intimate knowledge of how the other person ticks, not to mention the intense sexual chemistry. Harper and Logan could recall the good times as well as the bad. But as they get to know each other all over again, a decade after their split, they learn new things about the other person. This pushes them into irresistible old habits. But indulging their chemistry is one thing, forgiving and trusting again another matter entirely.

Hope you enjoy.

Love,

JC

MANHATTAN MARRIAGE REUNION

JC HARROWAY

MEDICAL ROMANCE

Harlequin®
MEDICAL
ROMANCE

Recycling programs for this product may not exist in your area.

ISBN-13: 978-1-335-94292-0

Manhattan Marriage Reunion

Harlequin Enterprises ULC
22 Adelaide St. West, 41st Floor
Toronto, Ontario M5H 4E3, Canada
www.Harlequin.com

Printed in U.S.A.

Lifelong romance addict **JC Harroway** took a break from her career as a junior doctor to raise a family and found her calling as a Harlequin author instead. She now lives in New Zealand and finds that writing feeds her very real obsession with happy endings and the endorphin rush they create. You can follow her at jcharroway.com and on Facebook, X and Instagram.

Books by JC Harroway

Harlequin Medical Romance

A Sydney Central Reunion

Phoebe's Baby Bombshell

Buenos Aires Docs

Secretly Dating the Baby Doc

Gulf Harbour ER

Tempted by the Rebel Surgeon
Breaking the Single Mom's Rules

Forbidden Fling with Dr. Right
How to Resist the Single Dad
Her Secret Valentine's Baby
Nurse's Secret Royal Fling
Forbidden Fiji Nights with Her Rival
The Midwife's Secret Fling

Visit the Author Profile page
at Harlequin.com for more titles.

To G, Thanks for our twenty-eight-year marriage,
inspiration for the HEA my characters are
always chasing. x

**Praise for
JC Harroway**

"JC Harroway has firmly cemented her place as
one of my favourite Harlequin Medical Romance
authors with her second book in the imprint and with
wonderful characters and a heart-melting and very
sexy romance set in the beautiful Cotswolds."
—*Goodreads* on *How to Resist the Single Dad*

CHAPTER ONE

UNDERNEATH HER SURGICAL mask Harper Dunn wore the serene expression she'd practised in the mirror and entered Theatre Six from the scrub room, her nerves stretched taut. Her locum position at Manhattan Memorial Hospital, or MMH, meant that seeing *him* was inevitable. Not that she had any intention of allowing one inconvenient ex-husband to stand between her and a coveted position as lead congenital heart surgeon at Manhattan's biggest hospital.

She glanced around the operating room, immediately spying the tall athletic build of Logan Grant. Even with his back to her and dressed in generic green surgical gowns, his stature and the way he carried himself were instantly recognisable. Of course, she'd once traced every inch of his body with her fingertips, her lips, her adoring kisses. But now that the time had come to actually face the man she'd once loved, a man she hadn't seen for ten years, she felt sick to her stomach.

A scrub nurse appeared before her, holding out a sterile gown.

'Thank you,' Harper said, trying to control her body's fight, flight or freeze response as she slipped her arms through the sleeves and pulled on sterile gloves. While the nurse tied her into the gown, Harper looked up, her eyes locking with Logan's.

'Dr Grant,' she said in a clear and unruffled voice, relieved to have got in the first word, even if she was struggling to breathe and speak at the same time. She might be over him, but he was still the last person to whom she wanted to show any hint of weakness. After mutually deciding to divorce and after Harper had fled to London to reinvent herself, they hadn't stayed friends.

'Harper,' he replied, the deep rumble of his voice reigniting long-forgotten memories: her name said a hundred different ways—with laughter, in frustration, on a passionate groan as he'd held her so tightly, she'd been certain they would last for ever, more fool her. She should have known better than to rely on love.

But Logan's voice also lacked surprise.

'I see you were expecting me,' she said. As a senior neonatal congenital heart surgeon at

Manhattan Memorial and acting clinical lead, Logan would, of course, know everything that happened in his department.

'I was,' he said with a tilt of his head. 'Welcome.'

No doubt he was also aware that she'd applied for a permanent job he probably already considered his. Too bad she was there to challenge his assumptions...

'Should we get the awkward personal conversation over with?' she asked, clasping her sterile hands together in front of her as she joined him near the monitors used to display the patient's scans and X-rays. 'Or shall we skip straight to discussing the patient before he arrives?'

The corners of Logan's brown eyes crinkled as if he was smiling beneath his mask. The expression was so familiar, it triggered an automatic download of memories from the four years they'd been a couple. Their electric first meeting at a medical school party, the triumphant smile on his face when she'd agreed to marry him a mere two years later, his look of defeat when he'd finally accepted their two-year marriage was over and reluctantly signed the divorce papers. But she hadn't taken it personally; Logan simply hated to fail.

'It's good to see you, Harper,' he said, catching her immediately off guard in his typically competitive way.

'Is it? Really?' she asked dryly, trying not to notice the new scattering of grey hair at his temples that only made him seem mature and distinguished, not older. No doubt he was regarded as something of a silver fox around MMH. He'd always been a classically tall, dark and handsome man.

'I find that hard to believe,' she added, forcing herself to stand close to him, as if he were just another colleague. 'Having your ex-wife apply for the permanent clinical lead position you want must surely be unsettling. I'll essentially be your senior. What a tricky professional dynamic that will be.' She looked up. She'd once loved that he was so much taller than her, six foot three to her five foot six. Now she resented his height advantage.

'If it comes to that...' he said evenly with a dubious raised brow. 'The job isn't yours yet. And just because we're in competition professionally, there's no need to come out fighting.' His eyes narrowed a fraction with the challenge she'd been expecting.

'How else can I make you understand that I'm no longer the old Harper,' she countered with a flick of a glance. 'The one who avoided confrontation at any cost, the one so madly in love with you I'd all but bent myself into the shape of a pretzel trying to fit into your world?' With his pretentious and wealthy family in particular.

'I never asked you to do that,' he said quietly, his stare intense.

'Don't worry,' she bluffed. 'Our divorce was good for me. Not to mention my time at the London Children's Hospital working with Bill McIntyre has considerably bulked out my CV. So I'd say the race for the clinical lead will be a fair fight.' Now that she was back, her ex needed to understand she was there to stay. Her father, Charlie, needed her.

'Well, in that case, may the best surgeon win,' he said, with his trademark confidence, something she'd once found wildly attractive when they'd first met, but now considered irrelevant.

Smirking, she congratulated herself. 'I see *you* haven't changed.'

'And you truly have?' he asked, fire glinting in the depths of his irises.

Because to look into his eyes was to remember the thousand times she'd made love to him, held him through his darkest times, laughed with him over life's little things and soaked up his beautiful smile like a wilting sunflower absorbs rain, Harper pretended to study the baby's radiological images. In truth, knowing that she'd be operating alongside Logan this morning, she'd already scoured the test results and patient files meticulously in preparation for this surgery *and* come in early to examine the baby and meet his concerned parents.

'Definitely,' she said. 'Unlike when we were married, I'm no longer a pushover, willing to tolerate things for an easy life. I've learned a lot about myself these past ten years.'

'Really? Did you learn that you're done with serious relationships?' he asked. 'Because *I'd* heard you were still single.'

Her mouth gaped open under her mask, her scowl blurring her vision. Trust Logan to get straight under her skin. 'Who from?' she asked, outraged, and then thought better of the question. 'You know what, don't bother answering that. My personal life is none of your business. And you know what they say—once bitten, twice shy. One ex-husband is enough for me.'

She met his stare, her chin raised defiantly as she fought her own rampant curiosity. Shamefully, she had occasionally cyber-stalked him over the years, keeping tabs on where he worked, telling herself that, one day, if she ever wanted to return to New York, he might become professional competition. Although she couldn't explain why she'd checked the marriage announcements, from time to time.

'How's Charlie?' he asked, changing the subject, as if he was doing a much better job of being unaffected by her than she was of him, as if they were two old acquaintances catching up, as if this hostile force field separating them was a figment of her imagination.

'My father is fine, thank you.' She glanced away. He didn't need to know that the main reason she'd returned to Manhattan was because her beloved dad, who'd never remarried after Harper's mother had left them both when Harper was ten years old, had developed brittle type 2 diabetes.

'And your family? Biddie and Carter?' she asked about his parents, more out of an attempt at nonchalance than genuine interest. She didn't wish the Grants ill. It had been Logan who'd far too often abandoned her to their stifling interference and expectations, which had played a big part in the demise of her and Logan's marriage. Growing up in Staten Island from a single parent family, Harper had never quite made the grade with the Grants, who came from old money, ran the most lavish charity galas the city had ever seen and owned large chunks of prime Manhattan real estate.

'They were well the last time I saw them, thanks,' he said, glancing at the anaesthetic room as if in search of their tiny patient. 'I'll let them know you asked after them.'

'Last time? Does that mean your parents have actually backed off from trying to run every aspect of your life?' She sniggered. 'Surely it can't be true…'

When they'd been together, his pushy, social-climbing parents had enjoyed throwing their money around, frequently suggesting influential allies they should meet, expecting the newly married couple at every high-profile social function the city had to offer. With such high expectations resting on his shoulders, Logan had grown up feeling as if he had something to prove. A career in medicine had been *his* choice, not theirs. The Grants had urged their eldest son to join the family business, a historic, billion-dollar real estate empire founded by Logan's great-grandfather that made the family a permanent fixture on the world's rich list.

'I run my own life,' he said looking mildly uncomfortable. 'But maybe we should discuss the case before our patient arrives.'

'Fine.' Harper wasn't there to become once more embroiled in Logan's elite brand of family drama. She had her dad to worry about, and Charlie Dunn only had Harper. 'But you don't need to worry; I'm well prepared. I've obviously reviewed baby Connor's case,' she said, eager to steer her thoughts away from her sudden flare of curiosity about her ex-husband. 'So I'm up to speed.'

She kept her eyes glued to the screen and on Connor's ECHO images, aware that Logan was close, too close for comfort. But it was time to forget that she'd once known everything about this man, to forget the painful past she'd left behind ten years ago and focus on the complex surgery ahead. 'Are there any particular complications you anticipate that we should discuss?'

In the induction room, the anaesthetist was prepping their tiny patient—a two-week-old boy with tetralogy of Fallot, a rare, life-threatening congenital heart malformation featuring a ventricular septal defect, pulmonary valve stenosis, a displaced aorta and an enlarged right ventricle.

'The ventricular septal defect is large,' Logan said, tilting his chin towards the images on the screen. 'But it should patch well.'

Harper nodded, sceptical that they could set aside their personal history and work together; something they'd never done before. 'Are you replacing the pulmonary valve or performing a valvuloplasty?'

'I prefer to decide once I've seen the anatomy,' he said, glancing sideways so she felt his eyes on her. 'What's your preferred method?'

Harper looked up sharply. The Logan she'd

known had been so self-assured, it had rarely occurred to him that opinions differing from his existed.

'I agree,' she said hesitantly, the words sticking in her throat. 'I like to decide once I'm in there. Although I can't quite believe you're asking for my opinion.'

Over the course of their tumultuous two-year marriage, there'd been little upon which they'd agreed. Where they lived—his apartment was bigger and better, thanks to his trust fund, with views of Central Park. Work compromises—at three years her senior, he'd qualified first and therefore had already begun to establish himself in a career before Harper. Family expectations—her father, Charlie, was an ordinary down-to-earth guy, a now-retired high school science teacher. By comparison, the Grants relished the glitz and glamour of Manhattan, always seen at the right parties with the right people, and had expected the same of their son and by extension, Harper, too. A young woman with eye-watering student debt and abandonment issues had stuck out like a sore thumb in their world, especially when Logan had regularly abandoned her to the social events in favour of his work.

'I'm glad we agree.' His eyes crinkled at the corners so she guessed he was smiling again.

'It should be plain sailing.' He glanced up as the anaesthetist finally wheeled their tiny patient into the room.

It was time to focus on work, on operating together for the first time. Telling herself that he was just another man, just another surgeon and that she owed him nothing beyond professional courtesy, Harper swallowed down her nerves.

'Which side of the bed do you prefer?' he asked, tilting his head in the direction of the operating table. 'From memory it's the left, but perhaps you *have* changed.'

Harper's face heated. Trust Logan to make some suggestive quip designed to remind her of their past.

'Oh, I've changed, plenty,' Harper shot back. 'But as you have seniority, *for now*,' she said pointedly, 'I defer to your preference. Of course, if I'm appointed as permanent clinical lead, that won't always be the case. So enjoy it while it lasts.'

His mask moved, his eyes smiling, and Harper looked away, relieved that she'd yet to see his mouth—the fullness of lips, the slanted curve of his smile, that dimple in his cheek. Wondering again at the wisdom of returning to the hospital where Logan worked, not that she'd had much choice—their chosen field was small, specialised and very competitive. She couldn't wait to be on the other side of this operation. To get away from him and gather herself. But with her eye on the prize of the job, Harper had no intention of being sidetracked by memories or friction with her ex-husband.

'Then let's do this,' he said with a decisive nod of his head that she recognised as a trait of the Logan of old. He positioned himself on the opposite side of the operating table from Harper so they could get to work, and Harper had never been more relieved to begin a complex surgery.

CHAPTER TWO

WITH BABY CONNOR'S surgery complete, and as the anaesthetist began to wake their tiny patient from the anaesthetic, Logan stretched out his back muscles and peeled off his gloves and mask, his glance drawn to Harper as it had been the very first time they'd met.

'Well, that went as smoothly as could be expected,' he said about the complex operation, surprised at how well they'd worked together, considering it was their first time and for all intents and purposes their divorce had made them enemies. But damn, she was a good surgeon, easily as good as him.

'Yes,' she said, tossing her garments into the laundry bin with the speedy efficiency that told him she planned to quickly make her escape. Now that the operation was over, the awkwardness from earlier had obviously returned.

But because of their history, it didn't feel right to let her simply walk away. If they were to be colleagues, surely they could be civil? After all, he'd never wished Harper any ill will, even after their divorce. In fact, he'd once loved this woman fiercely. Harper Dunn was the only woman he'd ever loved that deeply.

'Have you had a welcome tour of the hospital?' he asked, adding his gown and hat to the dirty pile while his heart pounded the way it had when he'd first invited her on a date.

'No,' she said, fresh wariness creeping into her voice. She kept her eyes downcast as she bent over the sink to wash her hands. 'But I'm sure I'll figure it out. One hospital is much like the rest.'

Logan took a sick kind of satisfaction from her response. 'Afraid to be alone with me?' he asked, joining her at the sinks and quickly washing up. 'I know we're both pretending to be unaffected by each other, but are we really fooling anyone, given our history?'

It would be easier if they could pretend their marriage had never happened, but even after ten years apart, if he allowed himself, he could still remember their good times, not just the bad—the passion, the laughter, the feeling that he'd found his soulmate. Maybe Harper could remember the good times, too.

'Don't be ridiculous,' she said, snatching some paper towels from the dispenser and drying her hands. '*I'm* not pretending at all, Logan. And why would I be afraid when I can hardly remember us; it was so long ago.'

'Ouch...' he muttered, rinsing his hands; he didn't believe a word of her speech. But he shouldn't goad her, not when he was trying to clear the air.

'And if my presence bothers *you*, do you really want more of my company?' she asked, turning to face him. 'Are you that much of a glutton for punishment?'

His first full, unobstructed view of her face in ten years punched a disturbing slug of heat through his stomach. She was still gorgeous; he should have expected *that*. She'd always had some kind of bewitching hold over him. Except her tied-back, long dark hair seemed richer than he remembered. Her golden-brown eyes with their thick lashes displayed all her emotions and sparked with predictable confrontation. And her lips... Full, soft looking with that pronounced cupid's bow, currently turned down in a frown. Why couldn't he for the life of him recall their taste?

Logan shrugged, acting casual while his heart raced. 'If we have to work together, who better than me, the department's acting lead clinician, to show you around? We need to find some way of working harmoniously together.'

But now he was regretting the offer. He didn't want to notice how physically, she still did it for him. Even with several weeks to prepare for her arrival at his hospital, she'd still somehow managed to throw him off balance. She *had* changed in some ways, as she kept reminding him. At thirty-seven, she was, of course, a little older, but she was still sharply intelligent and challenging and sexy as sin. Good thing he had work on which to focus.

'I guess we do need to be civil.' She smiled tightly. 'In that case, I'd love a tour. As long as it includes somewhere I can buy coffee.'

'That can be arranged,' he said, both relieved to have won her over and at the same time wishing he could simply ignore his ex-wife. Just because Harper was a beautiful woman he'd fancied the minute he'd seen her all those years ago, it didn't mean he was interested in making the same mistake twice. It had taken him a long time to get over her, after all.

'The hospital café is upstairs,' he said, holding open the door for her to pass through. His senses braced for that maddening light floral scent he'd immediately recognised even in the sterile environment of the operating room. It hit him anew, flooding his brain with memories. If he allowed himself to think about it, he could probably recall the name of that damned perfume. He'd bought it for her on more than one occasion during their relationship. But he'd spent ten years learning to forget his greatest failure in life: his divorce. He wasn't about to undo all that hard work in one morning.

Guiding her to the nearest flight of stairs, he forced his head to think about something other than how fantastic she looked and smelled. 'The fact that you have your goal set on a substantive post here must mean you're back in Manhattan for good?' He was fishing, but he'd always lived by the principle of *Know your enemy*.

While, after all these years, he still regularly met up for a beer with Charlie, Harper's dad, the two of them had made an unspoken agreement back at the start to rarely bring up Harper during their chats, which mainly centred on baseball and fishing. Charlie had of course, mentioned that Harper was returning from London, adding that she'd never managed to find love again after him, but Logan had breezed over it. Now he wondered if Charlie had ever told his daughter about his ongoing relationship with his ex-son-in-law.

'I'm afraid I am,' she said, shooting him another of those challenging looks that were both new and somehow also familiar. She certainly seemed more driven and ambitious, but still as self-sufficient as always. That aspect of her personality had given him the most grief when they were a couple.

'But surely you would never back down from a little healthy competition?' she added.

His pulse accelerated. Was she deliberately making this race for the job more exciting? She must remember his competitive streak. Dismissing the idea as irrelevant, he smiled. He wouldn't be flirting with his ex-wife, and when it came to competitions, he always won.

'Of course not,' he said. 'And the Harper I once knew was a great doctor. Whichever of us MMH appoints as clinical lead, they'll be getting a world-class surgeon.'

'I see your arrogance hasn't changed in the past ten years,' she said dryly, ignoring his compliment and entering the café on the hospital's ground floor.

'Like you, I've changed plenty, Harper,' he said, quietly, taking a deep, calming breath as they joined the queue. 'Clearly we're going to have to get to know each other all over again.'

After all, their work was intense and specialised, and just like this morning, often necessitated collaboration. The neonatal surgical team was tight-knit, the smaller congenital cardiac surgery team even more so.

'I'm not sure that's necessary,' she said primly as if horrified by the suggestion. 'I know all I need to know in order to effectively do my job, which is all I'm interested in.'

Logan huffed mirthlessly, his composure unravelling. 'There really is no need to keep beating me over the head with how uninterested you are in me as a person. I get it. It's loud and clear. But you know, if you want me to believe you're truly over me, no regrets whatsoever, you might want to consider dropping the hostile attitude, otherwise, it doesn't quite ring true.'

At his reminder of their past, her stare filled with momentary alarm, but she quickly composed herself. 'I knew you hadn't changed,' she challenged, somehow managing to look down her nose at him as she gave him the once-over. 'You're as egotistical as ever, always needing to win. No wonder there's no new wedding ring on your finger…'

His temperature spiked, half annoyance, half excitement. Despite her coolly indifferent act and her predictable jibes, she was just as curious about his personal life as he was about hers. 'It's like you said—one divorce is enough.' He shrugged, faking detachment, when really this woman had always had a knack of getting under his skin. That was one of the reasons their sex life had been so good. There was no fire without a spark.

'And you're right,' he added, 'I do intend to

win this particular race. Just because you and I have history, did you really expect I'd simply roll over and allow you to steal a job I've worked my entire career for?'

She fisted her hands on her hips. 'I've worked my whole career for it, too.' Her pretty eyes narrowed. 'Perhaps harder than you, because I'm a woman and because I don't have the privilege of your family connections.'

'There it is...' he muttered, stunned that the deep-rooted source of all their marital disharmony—their differences—had shown itself so early. Fool that he was, he hadn't expected their past resentments, their inability to communicate without lashing out, to resurface so quickly, especially not in the workplace. But no matter how changed she claimed to be, no matter how altered he knew himself to be, no matter how many years had passed, it seemed neither of them had fully resolved the issues that had ultimately led to their divorce.

'I'm not sure I like your insinuation, Dr Dunn,' he said, calmly. 'If I get the permanent clinical lead position, I will have earned it every bit as much as you.' Clearly their ability to rile each other up was one thing that *hadn't* changed.

'Right,' she said with a knowing nod of her head and mocking smile. 'Because your last name has never opened any doors. There's even a Grant Wing in this very hospital.'

Logan clenched his jaw in frustration. 'That was my great-grandfather's name as you well know,' he pointed out, tired of battling a legacy he'd never asked for. Even when his refusal to join the family business had almost caused his parents to disown him, he'd been determined to forge his own path. That's why he'd chosen a career in medicine.

'I can't help the family I was born into,' he added. 'The family you married into, I might add.' Once, a long time ago, she'd loved him enough not to care that he was a Grant.

She turned to face him, glaring, one hand on her hip, accentuating the hourglass shape of her figure, all but daring his gaze to dip to her breasts, her waist, her hips. 'Because I wanted *you*, not your family, although it often felt as if I saw more of your parents than I did of you.'

For an unguarded second, her comment about wanting him stunned him into silence, transporting him back to the early years of their relationship when they'd been crazy for each other and barely able to keep their hands off one another. He'd once loved this woman so fiercely, he used to watch her sleep, marvelling that she was his. But it had soured quicker than either of them had foreseen. They'd rushed into marrying, and he'd neglected her one time too many, although Harper, too, had played her part.

'Did you want me?' he asked, despite the guilt clouding his judgement. 'You had a funny way of showing it. It didn't take long after our wedding for the cracks to start and it wasn't all my fault. You kept shutting me out emotionally.' Each of them had struggled with their own demons. She'd withdrawn every time she was reminded of the fact that her mother had walked out when she was a kid. And he, out of a warped sense of guilt that he'd abandoned his family's business, had thrown himself into his surgical career, neglecting Harper and failing to set robust boundaries for his parents, tolerating way too much of their interference.

'I wasn't solely to blame, either,' she snapped.

'I never said you were.' He scrubbed a hand over his face. The last thing he'd wanted was to publicly air his dirty laundry for the other café patrons to hear. And he couldn't allow their past to interfere with their work, not when it so clearly led down the same dead-end street.

'Your parents took every opportunity to show us both how much they disapproved of your choice of a wife,' she continued, ignoring his comment. 'A motherless nobody from Staten Island was in no way suitable daughter-in-law material. They never liked me.'

'And yet I, too, wanted *you*,' he said quietly, his sense of defeat reignited from the ashes he'd spent the past ten years smothering.

She blinked up at him, a frown cinching her brows. With his pulse whooshing in his ears, the café around them, the other patrons waiting in line disappeared as they faced each other angrily, breaths gusting, eyes clashing.

'Can I help you, Dr Grant?' the woman behind the register said, snapping him back to the present. 'The usual, is it?'

While he and Harper had been pointlessly rehashing old arguments, they'd reached the front of the coffee queue. Logan tried to smile, recalling himself.

'I'll get these,' he said to Harper, stepping forward. 'I have an account here.'

But she was obviously having none of that. 'I'll get my own coffee, thanks,' Harper said, smiling at the bewildered server sweetly.

Logan reluctantly conceded and moved aside, frustration tensing his muscles.

'Listen, Harper,' he patiently said as she joined him in the wait for their coffees. 'Us working together was always going to be an adjustment.' One he'd thought he could handle. Now he simply hoped they could find some way of sharing a workplace without a full-blown war.

'An adjustment…?' she said, scoffing. 'We

can't make it half a day in each other's company without retracing well-worn paths paved with grudges and irritations.'

Logan pressed his lips together. She was right. Before he'd seen her again, he'd been confident he could leave the past in the past and work alongside his ex-wife as if she were any other colleague, but now he wasn't so sure.

'I think we should start again,' he went on. 'Our work is clearly important to us both. There's no place here for ego or one-upmanship. And how well we fit into a team environment will influence the admissions panel when it comes to appointing the clinical lead.'

'I agree,' she said haughtily, refusing to look his way. 'But this hospital tour was obviously a mistake. While we *have* to be colleagues, while we can put patients first and collaborate professionally, we clearly can't be *friends*.' She spoke the word with distaste, as if the idea of them ever getting along was unthinkable. 'There's too much history between us.' She looked up, her beautiful stare full of frustration and hurt, a flicker of vulnerability perhaps. Or maybe he imagined the latter.

'Maybe you're right,' he said with a sigh. 'After all, it wasn't friendship that brought us together.' That had been their mutual attraction, instantaneous, burning bright and hot.

'I suggest we simply focus on doing our jobs,' she said, her voice clipped. 'That's why *I'm* here. We cooperate when we must, but otherwise stay the hell away from each other. No more personal conversations. Because, when it comes to us, there really is nothing else left to say.'

Logan sighed again and bit his tongue. On some level, he had plenty he wanted to say. In the ten years he'd had to reflect on what had gone wrong in their marriage, he'd often wished he could go back in time and fix it. Instead, he'd lived with the guilt that he'd inadvertently neglected his marriage and hadn't stood up to his parents soon enough. He hadn't disabused them of all their fixed expectations, or fought against their pressures to conform and he hadn't protected Harper well enough. If he had, maybe, just maybe, he and Harper would still be together, because he'd never quite shaken the dissatisfaction of losing her.

'Maybe you should have thought about us having to avoid each other before accepting a locum position here,' he muttered, deflated. 'There are other hospitals.' Although MMH was the biggest, the neonatal cardiac surgery department the top statewide. And while physically he could try and keep his distance, he had a bad feeling that mentally she would occupy many of his thoughts now that he'd seen her again. After all, it had taken him years to forget her the first time around.

'I had no choice, believe me,' she snapped. 'I'm an only child. My father has never remarried and he's—' She broke off, her voice strangled with emotion as she looked away.

But then she'd always struggled to rely on him emotionally, something he attributed to her mother's abandonment, something that had made him feel so helpless while they were married. She had even less reason to confide in him now.

'Is Charlie the reason you came back?' he pushed, stunned because he liked and respected Charlie, considered him a friend. The last time they met he'd seemed fine.

She swallowed and collected herself, her reply reluctant. 'He's not well. I need to be close to him.'

Logan's mind reeled, the past instantly forgotten. 'I'm sorry. I had no idea. What's wrong? Is it serious?' He frowned and fought the instinct to reach out and touch her for comfort. He'd last seen Charlie a month ago. The older man had ordered a soft drink rather than his usual beer, saying he needed to lose a little weight, but Logan hadn't thought much of it given that Charlie had been his usual cheerful self. They'd discussed the Yankees latest win and their vacation plans before Charlie had let slip that Harper was coming back. He hadn't mentioned a word about his health.

'I don't want to discuss it,' she said, leaving the unspoken *least of all with you* coiled between them like razor wire.

'Okay,' Logan bit out, frustrated that he had more questions than answers. But given he was just an ex-husband she struggled to be in the same room with, his curiosity where Harper was concerned seemed utterly futile. He would ask Charlie directly.

In that moment, her coffee arrived. She took it from the barista with another smile that left him irrationally jealous. Once, a long time ago, before he'd let her down and taken her for granted, she'd smiled at him that way.

She was about to turn away when he touched her arm, halting her escape. He hated feeling helpless and shut out. But damn, her skin *was* as soft as he remembered, and this close, her eyes were even more beautiful. 'I'm sorry about Charlie. If there's anything I can do...'

'Thank you,' she said automatically as she eyed his hand on her arm with suspicion, as if he were contagious. 'I need to go. I'm meeting my resident, Jess, on the NICU.'

'Right.' Logan released her and nodded, frustration an itch under his skin. 'Well, rest assured that unless it's patient or work related, I'll keep my distance, as requested.' He'd do his best to ignore her. After all, treating her as just another colleague was unlikely to be anywhere near as hard as getting over her had been, and he'd survived that.

She looked up. 'Great.' A moment of hesitation seemed to hover in her gaze, but she pushed her shoulders back, that polite, indifferent mask falling over her features. 'Have a good day.'

With a sigh, he watched her leave the café, her ponytail swinging. Working together was one thing. They'd proved this morning that they could successfully collaborate when they needed to, even though she was still sporting a massive chip on her shoulder and a whole heap of resentment directed Logan's way. But forgetting about Harper Dunn, when she was still sexy enough to scramble his mind? He hadn't managed to achieve that these past ten years, so what hope did he have now that she was back in his everyday life?

CHAPTER THREE

PREDICTABLY, HARPER HADN'T slept well on her first night back. Aside from the successful surgery, her reunion with Logan had been as disastrous as she'd imagined. No matter how hard she'd tried to stay immune to him, and despite his insistence that he'd changed, Logan had still managed to worm his way under her skin. Their fight in the café had unsettled her. His accusation that she'd kept him out emotionally when they'd been together had played on her mind as she'd lain awake for hours. Even now, the next morning, she couldn't help but ruminate on her struggles with her feelings of abandonment throughout her teens and twenties. But what had been the point of talking about something she'd had no power to change?

As Harper and her fifth-year neonatal surgical resident, Jess, arrived on the NICU for a ward round, Harper resolved to shove Logan from her mind. Pausing at the sinks to wash her hands, she scanned the ward, her stomach sinking when she spied Logan and his resident, Greg, talking to some parents. He looked good out of scrubs. Urbane and professional. If she were a parent with a sick baby, she would absolutely trust his judgement.

That didn't mean she trusted *him*.

'Where do you want to start?' Jess asked as Harper finished drying her hands.

'As Dr Grant is already here, why don't we start on the other side of the ward.' Today was a new day. Ignoring Logan unless they were discussing work seemed the only logical plan, and it would help her to manage the unexpected and surprisingly strong resurgence of attraction.

She and Jess were just about to begin their ward round when an ear-splitting alarm sounded. They rushed to the crowded bedside, along with Logan and Greg. The nurses drew the curtains and Harper reeled to see the baby in distress was Connor, the patient she and Logan had operated on the day before.

A sense of panic descended. All four of them, as well as the neonatal nurses, worked side by side to assess the baby, checking tubes and electrodes, measuring vital signs and taking blood for analysis.

'Oxygen saturations have dropped,' Greg told them, adjusting the flow of oxygen through the baby's ventilator. 'But he's been stable over-night.'

With her panicked pulse bounding and her mind filtering the possible causes for Connor's respiratory distress, Harper glanced at the monitors, noting that the baby's breathing was rapid and his heart rate slow, the amount of oxygen in his blood alarmingly low.

Logan had his stethoscope in his ears, the bell held to the baby's tiny chest. Harper reached for her own stethoscope, placing it next to Logan's. Their fingers brushed in the confined space of the incubator, but there was no time to worry about that. At twenty-four hours post-op, any setback in Connor's recovery was extremely alarming.

After a few seconds, Logan looked up, his stare meeting Harper's, his concern evident.

'I think he has reduced breath sounds on the left,' Harper said, relieved to see Logan nod in confirmation that he'd heard the same thing. 'Possible pneumothorax.'

'I agree.' Logan nodded. Where yesterday had been about their divisions, now that their shared patient was in danger, they seemed to be united. Logan turned to both residents. 'Call Radiology for an urgent chest X-ray.'

Jess nodded and pulled out her phone, stepping away to make the call.

'Any fever?' Logan asked Greg, snapping on a pair of gloves.

Greg shook his head. A post-op infection would also need to be excluded, but a pneumothorax was more immediately life-threatening. The baby's blood pressure dropped and another alarm sounded.

'We don't have time to wait for an X-ray,' Logan said.

'I agree. Let's try to aspirate.' Harper reached for a sterile needle and syringe from a nearby trolley and passed them to him before quickly pulling on her own gloves. While Logan opened the packaging of the syringe, she swabbed the skin of the baby's left chest wall with an alcohol wipe.

'Thanks,' Logan nodded in gratitude. There wasn't much space for them both to work, but every second counted.

With the needle inserted into Connor's chest cavity, Logan pulled back on the syringe and removed twenty CCs of air that had escaped the baby's lung. Almost immediately, Connor's oxygen saturations improved, his blood pressure stabilising.

'Good call.' Harper released a sigh of relief, seeing the same emotion in Logan's expression. At least clinically, they were on the same wavelength.

'It could be a ventilation pneumothorax,' Logan said to the residents. 'But let's get a repeat ECHO to check the heart.'

'Are you okay to insert a chest tube?' Harper asked Jess, her mind spinning through a list of possible post-op complications.

Jess nodded and Greg said, 'We can do it together.'

Just then the radiographer arrived with the portable X-ray machine and with the baby stabilised for now, everyone moved aside for the radiographer to take the X-ray.

'Let Connor's parents know about the incident,' Harper said to his NICU nurse. 'Reassure them that Dr Grant has treated Connor and he's stable now, but either myself or Dr Grant will speak to them and explain everything when they come in.'

Logan peeled off his gloves and headed for the sink to wash his hands and Harper followed.

'Are we missing anything?' she asked Logan as she washed up, her pulse still racing away. 'I checked on him last night before I left, and he was stable.' Their work came with a high burden of responsibility, and she wouldn't be human if she didn't feel it sometimes. When your patients were so tiny and vulnerable, those alarms, which usually indicated something serious, were terrifying.

'I checked him, too,' Logan said, glancing her way so she saw both reassurance and lingering worry in his stare. 'His observations have been stable overnight. We were both happy with how the surgery went.'

She nodded, grateful that, for this patient, the responsibility was shared. Even if their personal grudges were unresolved, they could at least be cooperative at work. She'd seen yesterday how Logan was indeed a world-class surgeon. She couldn't begrudge him her professional respect. And there was something about watching him interact with tiny babies that was…unsettling. Perhaps it was just that once, a long time ago, she'd imagined herself having *their* babies.

'Common things are common,' he went on, logically. 'Let's suspend our concerns until we have the test results back.'

'You're right.' Harper swallowed, only partly reassured. Logan was the last person she'd thought she'd look to for any kind of support. But just because she trusted his clinical judgement, didn't mean she'd changed her mind about them being friends. For one, their chemistry was still pretty potent, and secondly, they'd proved yesterday that they couldn't be trusted to have any kind of personal conversation without bickering.

Harper hesitated, also recalling how yesterday, when he'd touched her arm and offered to be there for Charlie, she'd almost embarrassed herself with the sting of tears in her eyes. It had been a long time since Harper had relied on anyone but herself emotionally. She'd learned the hard way, when her mother left and again when her marriage had fallen apart, that relying on others was a sure-fire way to be hurt and let down.

'Why don't we leave Jess and Greg to liaise over the test results,' Logan added as they dried their hands side by side, that prickly wariness between them building. Clearly their residents were used to working together, even if *they* weren't.

But what had she expected? She'd told him to leave her alone unless they were discussing a patient or operating together.

'One of us can review Connor again in light of any new findings,' he added. 'I'm happy to do that, unless you want to.' He met her stare. His was wary.

'I'm sure that neither of us will be satisfied unless we've reviewed him again. It doesn't really matter which of us gets around to it first.' Harper looked back to where their residents stood at Connor's bedside in close conversation. *Very* close conversation, their whispering and body language stating they were way more intimate than two colleagues in the same department.

'Are they a couple?' Harper asked Logan, her curiosity getting the better of her. Technically, talk about their residents' personal lives wasn't work related, so she was kind of breaking her own rules. But as the newest team member, she didn't want to be out of the loop.

Logan followed the direction of her stare with his own. 'Yes,' he said, that same gaze landing on Harper. 'Young love. Do you remember what it felt like?'

Harper stiffened and then before she could stop herself, scoffed. 'Vaguely...' she lied, returning her glance to the couple. 'I hope for their sakes they don't learn the hard way how fleeting love can be. How it's better to rely on yourself, make your own happiness.'

She looked up at him defiantly, needing to remind him and herself that yes, the love they'd shared in their twenties had been intense and optimistic, but she and Logan couldn't forget where they'd gone wrong, or how quickly that love had disintegrated.

'They seem pretty solid,' Logan countered, his eyes flashing with challenge. 'In fact, they're engaged.' His eyes dipped to her mouth and she self-consciously licked her lips. 'If you stick around MMH, you might even receive an invitation to the wedding in a few weeks.'

Stepping away, he balled his paper towels and aimed them at the bin.

Harper pursed her lips in annoyance, galled that he seemed more relaxed than her about discussing the past. 'I told you I'm sticking around, and I told you why.' They were veering back into personal territory, but she'd been the one to initiate this topic of conversation.

At her reminder, a small frown cinched his brows together. 'Is Charlie okay?' he asked again. 'I messaged him last night but I haven't heard back yet.'

Harper's jaw dropped in astonishment. 'You messaged my father?'

'Yes.' Logan shrugged, slinging his hands casually into the pockets of his pants. 'I was worried about him after what you said. Is that so hard to believe? Do you have such a low opinion of me?'

Harper frowned, shaking her head, reluctant to acknowledge that her ex was a decent human being. But of course he was. He was a doctor, and just like it had yesterday in the hospital café, his concern for Charlie seemed genuine. It would be churlish of her to keep Charlie's news from him, even if she and Logan couldn't be confidants.

'He's been diagnosed with type 2 diabetes,' she said, reluctantly. 'He has a glucose monitoring device and is on insulin, but it's proving quite difficult to manage. There's no need for you to worry.'

As she spoke, Harvey's frown deepened and he crossed his arms over his chest, one hand stroking his clean-shaven chin in that thoughtful way of his. 'I'm shocked to hear that,' he said, stepping closer and dropping his voice to a more intimate level. 'I saw him not long ago, and your father has always been so healthy and active.'

'My grandmother was diabetic,' she said confused that he seemed to know Charlie so well. 'Bad genes, I guess. Where did you see him?' She was supposed to be avoiding personal conversations, but if her father and her ex-husband had talked about her, she wanted to know.

Logan's expression remained calm and resolute, as if he had nothing to hide. 'I met up with him in Brooklyn. We went out for a beer, although he didn't drink alcohol. Now I understand why.'

Harper gaped, thrown off balance once more because the older Logan seemed full of surprises. 'You met my father for a beer?' she asked, incredulous. Why? Had they done that before? And did they talk about her?

Logan nodded, his expression perfectly relaxed. 'Yeah, we've been meeting up every month for the past ten years. Charlie and I have always got along,' he said simply, his stare boring into hers.

Suddenly, there didn't seem to be enough air. 'I can't believe this,' she muttered. 'You've stayed in touch with my father since the divorce?' What kind of man did that? She'd assumed that, like her, he'd want nothing more to do with her, her family or any reminders of what they'd once meant to each other after their split. Now it seemed she was wrong. While she'd run away to London to forget him, he'd carried on his relationship with her father as if they were still together.

'Yeah.' Logan nodded, staring at her in that intense way of his.

Harper reeled. Why had her father never told her? Perhaps because after the divorce, she'd needed a fresh start. She'd moved to London and refused to talk about her ex, even with Charlie. After all what was the point? It had been over.

'What do you talk about?' she asked in spite of her better judgement, her stomach twisting with a discomfort she couldn't name.

'I could tell you,' Logan said, 'but as it's not work related, you've forbidden it.'

She scowled up at him, bound by a rule of her own making.

Logan checked his watch. 'I'm sorry, I need to get on with the rest of my ward round.'

Harper nodded, more confused than ever. 'Of course. Me too.'

He paused beside her and leaned close so she was bathed in that cologne of his. 'Please send Charlie my regards.' He raised his hand to catch Greg's attention, then looked down at Harper. 'And if you ever decide that you want to talk about us after all, you know where to find me.'

He headed across to the other side of the NICU, where Greg was waiting. All Harper could do was watch him go and feel horribly confused. How had she once more been lured into a personal conversation when she'd insisted that they only speak to one another about work? And how, when she was determined to come out on top in all her dealings with her ex-husband, did she feel as if he'd somehow gained the upper hand?

CHAPTER FOUR

TWO DAYS LATER, at the end of a long day, Logan was in the small room on the NICU designated for performing procedures on babies too unwell to leave the department, when Harper and Jess arrived.

'It is okay if Jess and I observe?' Harper asked, slipping on a mask from a box by the door. Her voice was wary but she didn't need to be there; she'd come by choice.

'Of course,' Logan replied, his gaze drawn to hers and his heart leaping excitedly. After the emergency on the NICU with baby Connor, they'd successfully steered clear of one another, only speaking when necessary about the patients in their joint care. That hadn't stopped Logan from constantly thinking about Harper or searching for a glimpse of her around the hospital. 'Why don't you scrub in,' Logan said to Harper, 'in case I need an extra pair of hands.'

Yes, things between them were…tense, but Logan trusted her as a surgeon.

'Okay,' she said as if eager to be involved. She donned a lead apron, washed her hands and slipped into a sterile gown and gloves.

Jess stood with Greg near the radiographer, where they could see the monitor and the images of the cardiac catheterisation procedure but were away from the sterile zone. Harper stood opposite Logan, the patient between them.

'This is three-week-old Alex,' Logan said. 'He has a PDA.' Patent ductus arteriosus was a condition that allowed the redirection of too much blood to the lungs. The vessel was important in the foetus, as the mother was breathing for her baby. Normally, it closed soon after birth, but sometimes, as in Alex's case, it failed to shut.

'So far, it's been resistant to non-invasive treatments,' he went on. 'So I'm attempting a PDA occlusion, today.'

'It's resisted first and second line drugs?' Harper asked, studying the images from the baby's most recent ECHO on an overhead screen, which showed the abnormal blood flow from his heart and the size of the abnormal vessel connecting the two major arteries leaving his heart.

'Yes.' Logan nodded. 'He's currently a high-risk candidate for open-heart surgery, and he's showing signs of worsening lung function.' The transcatheter procedure was technically less invasive than surgery, but all procedures carried risk. And the most common side effect with this approach was bleeding.

'So will you be using an occluder or a vascular plug?' Harper asked about the device he would insert into the abnormal vessel between the baby's aorta and pulmonary artery.

'I prefer an occluder,' he replied, glancing at the anaesthetist, who gave the all-clear to begin the procedure. 'Right, if everyone is ready, let's get started.'

With the anaesthetist and the neonatal nurse monitoring the baby's vital signs—pulse, blood pressure, oxygen saturation and respiratory rate—Logan used the ECHO probe to locate the baby's femoral artery and vein in the groin. With the vessel located, he passed a guide wire into the vein, slowly feeding it along the vessels towards the heart.

He paused intermittently, and the radiographer displayed the position of the tip of the guide wire with real-time X-rays and the use of fluoroscopic dye that outlined the blood vessels.

'Right,' Logan said to the residents observing. 'I'm going to insert the occlusion device now.' Trying not to hold his breath, he slowly and carefully fed the device along the guide wire. With the occlusion device in the correct location lying across the abnormal connection, or ductus, he took one final X-ray to ensure he was happy with the position.

'Looks like a good placement,' Harper said, as she scrutinised the image and then glanced his way encouragingly.

Logan nodded, happy with the images. Slowly, he began to withdraw the guide wire. That was when the baby's heart rate shot up, triggering an ear-splitting alarm.

Logan froze, his eyes darting to the heart monitor, which showed an abnormally fast heart rate.

'Ventricular tachycardia,' the anaesthetist said, jerking to his feet. 'Blood pressure is falling.'

Adrenaline shot into Logan's system. The abnormal heart rhythm meant the heart was beating too fast to be effective. As both he and Harper tried to locate a pulse, her eyes met his.

'Nothing,' she said. 'You?'

Logan shook his head, his stomach sinking. 'He's in cardiac arrest.'

Shifting positions, Harper placed her hands around the baby's chest so her thumbs met over his sternum and commenced cardiac compressions. Logan quickly reached for the defibrillator, charging the device to deliver an electrical shock to the baby's heart.

'Clear,' he said, waiting for Harper to remove her hands. He placed the paddles on the baby's chest and delivered the shock.

With his pulse a deafening roar in his head, Logan stared at the heart monitor. It took a second or two, but then the heart returned to a normal, sinus rhythm. Logan all but sagged with relief. To check, he placed his fingertip in the baby's opposite groin, feeling the reassuring beat of the femoral pulse.

'Blood pressure recordable again,' the anaesthetist said, the tension around the room easing as everyone breathed normally once more.

Logan swallowed hard, the close call rattling him so his insides trembled from the adrenaline rush. Cardiac arrest were two of the most terrifying words when it came to their tiny and vulnerable patients. This procedure should have been relatively routine and less risky than open-heart surgery, but he knew from experience that he always needed to be ready for anything. Cardiac arrhythmias were more common in babies with congenital heart disease. And while this one might have been triggered by the procedure, Logan hadn't done anything wrong. That didn't stop the sudden flare of inadequacy the emergency had brought on.

'Well done,' Harper whispered as he looked up to see his relief was mirrored in her eyes. Surgeon to surgeon, she was offering support, but because of their personal history, because she'd whispered her words as if for his ears only, her praise felt somehow intimate. And with things between them so…prickly, he wasn't prepared for that.

'Is everyone happy to proceed?' he asked, breathing through the feeling of responsibility. The buck *did* stop with him. This was his patient and he was the acting clinical lead in the department.

With the nod from the anaesthetist and catching the same from Harper, Logan continued to slowly withdraw the guide wire, completing the procedure without further incident.

'Let's run some blood tests,' he told Greg as he pulled off his gloves and mask, trying to hide how rattled he still felt. His resident nodded and set about taking a sample from the baby's central venous line.

'Can you order a repeat ECHO,' Harper asked Jess, who nodded and accessed the computer in the corner of the room.

'Keep an eye on Alex's urine output,' Logan told the neonatal nurse. 'And I want thirty-minute observations until further notice.'

As the nursing staff prepared baby Alex for

a return to the NICU, Logan removed his gown and made a note of the procedure in Alex's file. Rationally, he knew that this could happen to anyone, including Harper, but for some reason, he couldn't look her way. He felt too raw. And instinct told him she would know exactly how he was feeling because of their history. Just like he knew her, she knew him. And with their past hurts unresolved, he didn't want her to see him when he was feeling so vulnerable.

'I'll go and speak to Mum and Dad,' he told Greg, before leaving the room and heading for the NICU family room. As he walked, he reasoned away his reaction. As his wife, Harper had once known him better than anyone. Would she still know that he struggled to tolerate failure, whether it was in his personal life or at work? He knew where that perfectionist trait came from: his parents' constant expectations while he'd been growing up. And when it came to Harper... He considered losing her his biggest failure of all. That was something he definitely didn't want her to know.

With baby Alex stable and recovering on the NICU after his procedure, Harper was thinking about leaving the hospital for the night, when her feet paused outside Logan's office. She loitered in the corridor, her heart thudding erratically and her stare fixed on his closed door. Was he still there or had he already gone home?

Because she'd once known him so well, and because he was still essentially the same person with the same values, she'd immediately recognised how shaken by the cardiac arrest he'd been earlier. She would have felt the same if she'd been the one performing the procedure. Everyone in that room had felt that sense of panic and urgency. Losing a baby was the worst part of their job.

She dragged in a breath, torn between keeping her word and staying away or making sure he was okay. Logan was a good surgeon, but he'd always been driven and uncompromising. No doubt he'd be meticulously analysing what he could have done differently right about now. But it was none of her business how he dealt with the tougher psychological aspects of their work. So why couldn't she just walk away?

Deciding it was best to show she was a team player, clear her conscience and check up on him she tapped on the door. Maybe she felt compelled because he'd offered her support over Charlie's diagnosis, or because he'd been constantly on her mind this week. Or maybe it was simply that their past history gave them a connection that was almost impossible to ignore and if she simply went home without ensuring he was okay, she'd only ruminate and worry her way through another sleepless night.

She held her breath, second-guessing the impulse. He wouldn't necessarily want her reassurance anyway, not when things between them were so…complicated. She was just about to walk away, deciding that he wasn't in his office after all, when the door opened.

He stood framed in the doorway, his tie removed, his top few shirt buttons undone and his dark gaze haunted.

'Hi…' she said, her throat tight. 'I just wanted to check you're okay before I left for the night.'

Memories of when he'd lost his beloved grandfather slammed into her. Back then, she'd held him throughout a long, sleepless night, silently making love to him in the pre-dawn, loving him so hard she could never have predicted that her feelings would end. Now the instinct to touch him was so strong she curled her fingers into fists. The thing that had been niggling at her for the entire week she'd been back nudged at her mind again. She didn't really know this older version of Logan even though she recognised traits of his similar to the man she'd once loved. He *had* changed. He was older and more confident, not that he'd ever had problems in that area. But he seemed more comfortable in his skin.

'Come in,' he said, inviting her into his office, which had a desk, a sofa and even a kitchenette with a sink and bar fridge.

Harper closed the door, her hands twisting together helplessly. Maybe this had been a mistake. She was supposed to be steering clear of him.

'It could have happened to anyone, Logan,' she said, sensing his doubts, knowing he'd be hard on himself because he hated to fail. 'We've all been there. I hope you're not blaming yourself.'

Logan winced, turning away from her. 'Would that knowledge make *you* feel any better if you'd been the one in charge of the procedure?' He took two bottles of water from the fridge and passed one to Harper, avoiding eye contact. 'Would it help when you had to explain to the frantically worried parents how their baby's heart had stopped under your care?'

Because her legs felt shaky, Harper sat on the edge of the sofa. 'I guess not,' she admitted in defeat. 'But you push yourself harder than most people. At least you used to…' The more she learned about this older Logan, the less certain she was that she'd ever known the smallest thing about him, other than how he'd made her feel cherished at first, and then later on in their relationship, lonely, abandoned, inadequate. Or maybe she'd made herself feel that final way, because of her mother...

'It's not that I push myself,' he said, wheeling his desk chair from behind the desk to sit opposite her. 'I just...hate to fail.'

Harper shrugged and smiled sadly. 'Same difference.' His admission surprised her. They weren't able to be friends, only exes and colleagues. The Logan she'd been married to had often struggled to be vulnerable or express his feelings, thanks to his parents' expectations. Because of her abandonment issues, she'd been the same, so she hadn't pushed him too hard. Back then, they'd both locked part of themselves away.

'Anyway,' he said, unscrewing the lid of his bottle and taking a swallow, 'I thought we weren't allowed to discuss the past.' He was looking at her in a way that made her all too aware they were alone, late at night, the hospital around them quiet with only a skeleton staff on the night shift.

'We're not.' She looked down at her lap. 'I'm just checking up on a colleague after an alarming emergency. That's work related. And you'd do the same if it had been me running the procedure.'

'I would,' he said with a decisive nod. Something shifted between them as they stared at each other in awkward silence, the seconds ticking by. Harper fought the urge to squirm under his scrutiny while her heart galloped.

'Perhaps this was a mistake,' she said finally, placing her untouched bottle of water on the table and rising to her feet. 'I shouldn't have disturbed you. Sorry.'

She no longer knew this man, and because of the past, it wasn't her place to offer advice or comfort. Why would he want that from her, just like she wouldn't seek it from him? But his friendship with Charlie was…confusing.

He stood, too, their bodies closer than she'd have liked. 'I'm glad you stopped by,' he said, his glance shifting over her face. 'I've been wanting to talk to you. I don't think our agreement is working. I'd like to revise it.'

'Of course you would,' Harper said, unsurprised. 'What about it isn't working?' She raised her chin, looking up at him. His height and the cramped space meant he filled her vision, a perspective that left her jittery. It had been a long time since she'd been this close to him and alone.

'When I agreed to steer clear of you, I hadn't properly considered all the practicalities,' he said. 'With us seeing each other all the time around the hospital, with us working so closely together, things have been…playing on my mind.'

'What kind of things?' she asked cautiously, preparing for another disagreement.

'Well firstly,' he said, 'I'd like to clear the air and apologise for your first day.'

Harper started, blinking up at him, shocked into silence by his willingness to admit fallibility.

'I wasn't quite as prepared to see you again as I'd hoped I'd be,' he added, his eye contact unwavering despite him admitting he'd been nervous to see her. 'And obviously those past resentments are still there and need addressing. It certainly wasn't my intention to dredge up the past. It's like you said—ancient history. Like it or not, I had to get over you a long time ago.' His eyes bored into hers, as if he was forcing himself to prove the truth of his words.

Like it or not…?

Harper held her breath, more confused than ever. 'I got over you, too,' she said, unable to keep the challenge from her voice. But exactly how hard had it been for him to forget her? She'd assumed he'd moved on pretty quickly. After all, their entire relationship, their marriage certainly, had been brief. But now she'd not only discovered that he'd kept in touch with Charlie, but that he'd maybe struggled to let go of their relationship. These new revelations were messing with her head.

'And I did my fair share of dredging that first day,' she added. 'I'm a big girl. I can own up to my share of the blame, but I really didn't come here to talk about us.' Not when she was desperately trying to ignore the fact that they'd ever been a couple in order to manage her confusion at still finding him attractive, familiar but also foreign.

'I know,' he said, his eyes hardening. 'And I know we can't be friends. But that emergency earlier has proved that we can't simply operate as colleagues, either, separately going about our business. If you're staying on at MMH, we'll see a lot more of each other, whichever of us gets the job as clinical lead. I'd like to think we're mature enough to move past the fact that we used to be married, a long time ago.'

Harper hesitated, her brain snagging on how it had felt to be married to him. When times were good, they were amazing together, but she'd learned over the years not to torture herself with those particular memories. What was done, was done. She'd had to learn that when her mother left.

'So in the hopes of clearing the air between us,' he went on, 'I want to apologise, again.'

Harper frowned, her pulse whooshing in her

ears. 'What for?' The old Logan had been un-compromising, bordering on arrogant, rarely admitting he was wrong.

For a second, doubt shifted over his expres-sion. 'I let you down as a husband,' he said, holding her eye contact so her breath caught. 'I've always regretted that. Like I said, I hate to fail.' A ghost of a smile tugged at his mouth, and for an unguarded moment, Harper longed to see one of his genuine, full-blown smiles. Logan had an amazing smile.

'I...' She faltered. Stunned that he had re-grets, and even more stunned that he'd admit them to her of all people, Harper blinked re-peatedly, searching for the right words. 'You can't take all the blame,' she said, breathing hard. 'Our marital implosion was a joint effort. I didn't enjoy feeling second place to your ca-reer or being managed by your parents. It made me feel constantly inadequate. But my thirties have been all about learning that conflict isn't fatal. That I can hold my own, state my opin-ion calmly and decisively, rather than backing down, saying nothing and then feeling resent-ful.' Maybe they'd both do things differently now that they were older and wiser...

'I guess we were both dealing with things,' he said, tilting his head. 'Maybe we rushed into marrying because I had to start work while you were still a medical student.' He scrubbed a hand over his face so he heard the rasp of his facial hair, and she wondered how it would feel against her skin. 'Since you left, I've learned to take full ownership of my life and admit my flaws. Losing you certainly helped me to come to terms with the fact that I'm not ever going to be the perfectly moulded son my parents wanted.' He shrugged, his eyes hardening. 'Needless to say, they're still processing that reality. But it's no longer my problem.'

It came then, the smile she'd secretly craved, cautious at first, most likely because they had so much history and so much time had elapsed since they'd trusted each other. But just because this was the most honest conversation they'd ever had, she didn't need to trust him to work with him.

As his lips stretched wider, her stare snagged on his sexy mouth. That he'd changed, that he harboured regrets made no difference now. It was too late for them. And there was still a part of her desperate to cling to those past resentments. To let go of them fully would force her to acknowledge how little her attraction to this man had waned over the past ten years. Rationally, it made sense. Their insatiable chemistry, their healthy sex life had been the one area of their marriage that worked without effort. That didn't mean she had any desire to relive the past or fall back into old patterns.

'We don't have to talk about this,' she croaked out almost pleadingly. 'We're obviously both feeling emotional after the scare of the cardiac arrest, and it's late. It's been a long day in a busy week.' Emotional decisions were always open to regret and she couldn't afford to have regrets where Logan was concerned.

He nodded, his eyes glittering. 'I'm not denying that, but I think we need to talk sometime, Harper. About us. About what went wrong. Don't you ever think about it?'

Static buzzed in Harper's ears. How often did *he* think about it? 'Maybe...'

Maybe it wouldn't hurt to talk. Maybe it would help them both to lay the past to rest.

'But not tonight,' she finished.

That *he* had regrets, that he might be stuck in the past added to her desperation to get away from the way he was making her feel, as if they could wipe the slate clean and start again. It would suit her better if they left their messy past *in* the past. Only there were elements of their relationship still very much rooted in the present, like their chemistry. No matter how hard she tried to ignore that, it constantly knocked her off balance.

'I should go,' she said, wrapping up the conversation as she glanced at the closed door. But her feet felt welded to the carpet.

'Thanks for checking on me.' He shifted his body, stepping closer still.

For a terrifying and exhilarating second, he looked like he might lean in and kiss her cheek. Acting on some kind of long-forgotten instinct, Harper responded, meeting him halfway, her conflicted thoughts finally falling silent as their lips touched.

Time sped up as exhilaration shot through her. His hands cupped her face and pulled her close. She rested her palms on his chest and surged up onto her toes, intercepting his passionate kiss as if it was the most natural thing in the world. To some extent it was. He might seem like a completely new man, but he was also achingly familiar. Just Logan. And he'd once been everything to her.

Harper's pulse bounded harder as his lips slid over hers, coaxing, chasing. His arms banded around her back so she was crushed against his hard chest. The well-known scent and heat of him washed over her like some sort of intoxicating love potion, drugging and entrancing, making her forget.

But she *didn't* love him any more. This was simply lust and poor judgement working hand in hand. Before her brain had a chance to snap out of its daze, his tongue surged against hers, turning her legs molten. As if acting on their own, her fingers tunnelled into his hair. She returned his kisses, losing herself for a moment in the good parts of their past. Moaning because it had been so long since she'd kissed anyone, and her body remembered this intense pleasure she'd only ever felt with Logan, craved it as if rebelling against the enforced abstinence she'd put it through in London, where she'd had only a couple of semi-serious relationships over the years.

But unlike those London men she'd optimistically dated off and on, she knew exactly where she stood with Logan. This meant nothing. They'd just done it so many times in the past their bodies remembered the moves. Muscle memory. And it was clearly a reaction to stress. A moment of madness that she'd put a stop to, any second. Unless he did first.

His hand found her breast and she gasped against his lips, darts of desire passing through her like lightning strikes. She needed to stop. She would, soon… His thumb brushed over her nipple through her clothes, and her body all but incinerated, liquid heat flooding her belly, her pelvis, her legs, leaving her unstable, so she clung to him.

'Harper…' he said after tearing his mouth

away, her name and his eyes full of questions for which she had no logical answers. His fingers continued to stroke her nipple, driving her insane with need. His lips trailed down the side of her neck and she felt the hardness of him against her belly. Her mind spun, reason fighting its way to the surface for breath. What was she doing kissing her ex-husband? And at work? Just because it felt good didn't mean it was a good idea.

With an effort that felt superhuman, she finally shoved him away; her heart beating so fast she couldn't seem to catch her breath. They faced each other, panting hard. Dark desire made his eyes almost black. She looked away, blocking out the sight of him aroused and confused, reluctant to see how much he wanted her, because to witness it would be to admit she wanted him, too.

'That was stupid,' she said, choking back the surge of longing. Her body remembered the sublime pleasure of being touched by him, whether her mind wanted it to or not. A part of her knew giving in to that pleasure would be good. She and Logan had always just clicked in the bedroom. But that alone hadn't been enough to save their relationship.

Logan scrubbed a hand through his hair and then dragged it over his face. 'Probably,' he agreed, stepping back, putting some distance between them. 'You should go.'

Probably...?

What did he mean by that? Did he want to revisit the past? Part of Harper was tempted, too, because it would just be sex, really good sex. Nothing else could ever happen between them, not when they'd previously been there, bought the T-shirt *and* left a scathing one-star review.

'It's been an emotional day,' she reasoned, needing some logical explanation for why she'd behaved so recklessly with her ex-husband of all men.

He nodded and turned away, placing himself behind his desk, as if he needed the physical barrier. 'You're right. Goodnight, Harper.'

He clearly didn't want to discuss it any further, and maybe he was right to simply ignore that incredibly foolhardy kiss. After all, what else was there to say? It had been a mistake, and together they'd already made enough of those.

'Goodnight,' she croaked, reaching for the door handle with a trembling hand, desperate now to get away from him so she could shake some sense into her head.

But as she left the hospital and headed home on the subway, her footsteps automatic, her mind was free to wander. No matter how hard she tried, she couldn't forget that thirty seconds of easily accessed and effortless pleasure. Because Logan was the only man to ever make her burn that way.

CHAPTER FIVE

THAT SATURDAY LOGAN attended a gallery exhibition in SoHo that his charitable foundation was sponsoring. He'd started the Edgar Grant Foundation with the money left to him by his grandfather. As a single man of forty, Logan had all but given up thinking about having a family of his own, reasoning that even if he had found another woman he wanted to start a family with after Harper, the last thing he wanted to do was to follow in his parents' footsteps when it came to overbearing parenting. Setting up the foundation enabled him to do some good in his community, to give back to the city that had benefited his family so much.

But having met the Reece Gallery owner and purchased a piece of art from one of the up-and-coming artists, his work there was almost done. As soon as he could escape Elliot Reece, a talkative bohemian gent in his late fifties who seemed fond of flamboyant waistcoats…

As the gallery owner talked, Logan's mind wandered to Harper and that incendiary kiss in his office. What a stupid mistake. Things between them had been tense enough before they'd succumbed to temptation. Now he had fresh memories of kissing her to add to the long list of past ones, and that was enough to keep him awake at night.

Looking up from his conversation, which was growing a little tedious even if he had been paying full attention, he immediately spotted Harper at the other end of the cavernous room. His pulse leapt at the sight of her. The noises around him, the conversations and background music fell silent as she became Logan's sole focus. She looked fantastic, wearing a little black dress, her hair styled in soft waves that kissed her shoulders. But more invigorating than how she looked physically, was the fact that she was laughing and smiling with one of the artists, a tall guy in his thirties. But what was she doing there? Was she on a date…?

Vicious jealousy winded Logan. The foreign feeling was reminiscent of the possessiveness he'd experienced in the early days of their relationship, but perhaps it made sense in light of that seriously hot kiss in his office two nights earlier.

'Excuse me,' he said to Reece, cutting him off

mid-sentence. 'I should probably mingle with some of the artists.' Having escaped, Logan made a beeline for Harper and her friend, his pulse accelerating with every step.

'I didn't know you were an art lover,' he said, as he joined them, and they both looked up.

Harper blinked, her cheeks flushing. Her lips, which were slicked with gloss, pursed as if she was annoyed to see him. 'Logan,' she said. 'What are you doing here?'

Her question dragged his mind from the inconvenient thought of how that one kiss had whet his appetite for more. A dangerous and pointless thought when she was standing there with another man. Not to mention that she was the last woman on earth Logan should be kissing, not that his body, his libido, seemed to give a damn.

'My foundation is sponsoring the exhibition,' he said, offering her friend his hand in greeting. 'I'm Logan Grant. Good to meet you.'

As he spoke, Harper made some hand gestures to the man and something tugged at Logan's memory.

'Logan, this is Jake Barrington,' Harper said, casting her friend an apologetic look and signing with her hands as she spoke. 'Jake is an old school friend of mine. You've actually met before, a long time ago.'

'Jake, of course,' Logan said with a smile, the pieces clicking into place. He *did* remember Jake, who was deaf and communicated by a combination of sign language and lip-reading. 'Congratulations on the exhibition,' Logan added to the other man, grateful to Harper for signing out his words. 'I love your work. I've actually purchased one of your pieces for my apartment.'

Jake signed thank you, and then they were interrupted by another man, who stole Jake away, leaving Logan and Harper finally alone. The air around them seemed to still.

'You started a foundation?' she asked, the scent she wore flooding his awareness so he noticed the shimmering make-up around her beautiful eyes. Damn, she looked good. *Too* good. Tempting.

'Yes. With the trust I inherited from my grandfather. I missed you at the hospital Friday,' he said, needing her to know that their kiss, the passion that they'd proved was just beneath the surface, had been constantly on his mind. 'Were you avoiding me?' he asked, noting how interested she seemed in the art lining the stark white walls all of a sudden.

'Don't be ridiculous,' she said, snagging a champagne flute from the tray of a passing server and taking a long swallow. 'Why would

I need to avoid you? I spent most of Friday in clinic.' She swept a dismissive gaze over him, but he wasn't fooled. She wasn't as indifferent as she would have him believe, and the pulse in her neck was going crazy.

'Because we kissed,' he said, simply, his lips buzzing as he recalled the delicious taste of her, familiar but also foreign because it had been so long. But oh, how they'd slotted back into place, like two sides of the same coin.

She glanced around nervously and then glared up at him. 'I told you, that was a mistake. One I don't want to talk about.'

Logan pressed his lips together. He'd been expecting her denial. But he knew her too well for her to hide her body's reactions. 'Maybe, or maybe it was just unfinished business.' he said, gratified to see her stare widening in alarm.

If she hadn't stopped him Thursday, if he hadn't unearthed the strength to say goodnight and watch her walk away, he might have slept with her, right there in his office, because their chemistry didn't seem to care that they were divorced.

'Unfinished business?' she asked, her voice breaking.

Logan nodded, stepped closer, aware that they were surrounded by people admiring the paintings and enjoying delicious canapés. 'Was there no part of you that still yearned for me after we walked away from our marriage?' He was so close, he heard her soft gasp and pushed on. 'I let you go ten years ago, Harper, but just because I signed the papers, it didn't mean it was totally over for me.'

When he pulled back, her face was slack with shock, her eyes swimming with desire and confusion. 'Don't say that,' she whispered.

'Then don't look at me that way,' he replied, his gaze tracing her unique and beautiful features. 'There's obviously something left between us, otherwise you wouldn't have kissed me back as if we'd never been apart. Don't forget, I know you. I know your body's responses were honest the other night, even if you're now trying to deny it, perhaps to save face.'

Her lips pursed in disgust. 'Maybe we just momentarily slipped back onto old habits, ones that as far as I'm concerned are also *bad* habits.'

Logan sighed, reluctant to get into another argument, but even more reluctant to walk away for some reason, probably because their chemistry was simply too hard to ignore. He'd tried and failed.

'So you haven't once thought about me in ten years? Is that what you're saying?' he asked. 'I don't believe you. And I still think we should talk and clear the air, because avoiding each other is clearly impractical. Manhattan clearly isn't big enough.'

She shook her head in disbelief, but she looked away tellingly. 'Believe what you like. I kissed you, but I don't owe you any of my thoughts or confidences. That ship sailed when you showed me where I stood in your priorities and left me alone to fend for myself with your parents, time after time.'

Logan winced, hating that she was right. He *had* prioritised his career when they were together, missing social events for emergency surgeries, pulling long hours to prove to himself and his parents that he'd done the right thing in championing his choice of career. 'That wasn't conscious on my part,' he said. 'But I had my reasons. For one, I thought you would understand the demands of our profession. But you're evading the point.'

'And what is the point?'

'That since coming back to New York, since kissing me like there was no tomorrow, you must have wondered if our chemistry is still as hot as it used to be. At least I can be honest about it. Maybe it's *me* who shouldn't believe a word *you* say.'

She raised her chin and looked down her nose at him. 'Don't they say that the definition of stupidity is doing the same thing over and over again and expecting a different outcome?' Her eyes glittered with challenge. 'I'm not stupid, Logan. I told you, I'm here for Charlie and for work. Just because my body remembered the steps, doesn't mean I have any intention of dancing.'

So she *had* thought about it. She *did* remember how good they were physically, not that it really mattered. He wasn't stupid, either. 'Maybe you're right. Neither of us wants to go there, no matter how good it would feel,' he muttered, defeated. 'So are you seeing Jake?' He couldn't help asking. He almost hoped her answer would be yes, so he'd have a solid reason to totally back off.

She laughed, a mirthless sound. 'No, he's a friend. An old friend. I'm not looking for a relationship at the moment, not that it's any of *your* business.' She made a point of ignoring him and sweeping her gaze around the room as if looking for someone. 'What about *you*? Where's your date? You don't want to be photographed for the society pages all alone.'

Now it was Logan's turn to scoff. 'If you're asking if I'm seeing anyone, the answer is no, but maybe you should have asked that before you kissed me.' In fact, it had been a while since he'd bothered with dating. Women his age expected a degree of time commitment that he couldn't often give because of his work. Of course, Harper now fully understood the demands of their job and shared his work ethic.

She shot him a venomous look.

'I'm here alone tonight,' he confirmed. 'And I don't care about social climbing. I never have.'

Hesitation clouded her gaze for a moment. Her eyes darted away once more, then her expression hardened, as if she were slipping on a mask of indifference. 'Maybe you don't care about appearances, but from what I remember, *they* do.' She tilted her chin, looking at someone behind him.

Logan turned and saw his parents, who had obviously just arrived at the exhibition. His stomach sank like a stone. He always kept his father abreast of the events supported by his charitable foundation, which after all, was named after Carter Grant's father. But his parents rarely attended, simply making a sizeable donation instead. He certainly hadn't expected them to turn up tonight, mainly because the Reece Gallery was small and situated on the wrong side of East Fifty-Ninth Street. But with perfect timing, here they were.

For a moment, Logan was transported back in time to other events, ones he and Harper had attended as a couple. In those days, Logan's parents had expected their attendance, as if they'd wanted to present a united Grant family front to the world. He'd known that Harper had felt out of her depth with his parents' snobby friends. She'd usually acted uncomfortable and withdrawn, and Logan had felt trapped in the middle, trying to appease both his wife and his parents, whom he'd left in the lurch by rejecting the family business. But the failure of his divorce had humbled him, sweeping away any need for pretence. Now, after losing the love of his life, he only pleased himself, even if it was too little too late for him and Harper.

Biddie and Carter scanned the room, spying him at once. They made their way over, their polite smiles faltering as they took in Harper, who had stiffened at his side. He half expected her to simply walk away from her ex-in-laws, but to her credit, Harper stood her ground.

'Mum, Dad… I wasn't sure if you'd make it.' He offered his parents a tight smile and shifted closer to Harper's side, fighting the temptation to put his hand at the small of her back in a clear and possessive demonstration of where his loyalties had always stood, even if he'd messed up and neglected to show Harper that in the past. 'I ran into Harper tonight,' he went on. 'She's recently returned from London and has joined us at Manhattan Memorial.'

Harper looked up at him sharply, as if surprised that he hadn't already told his parents she was back in the city. But, brought up with their emotionally distant style of parenting, Logan had never once confided in his parents about his divorce. And now, they needed to understand that he was only interested in rebuilding bridges with Harper, given they had to work together. He was determined that, one day, he and his ex-wife would also lay the past to rest.

Carter Grant recovered from his surprise first, swooping in to press a kiss to Harper's cheek. 'How are you, my dear?'

'I'm well, thank you. And you?' she asked, politely.

Carter Grant made some casual comment about getting older, to which Harper smiled. Logan's mother couldn't quite conceal her shock at finding Logan talking to his ex-wife, but she made a solid effort to cover it up.

'You look wonderful,' she told her ex-daughter-in-law. 'London obviously agreed with you. So are you back in Manhattan to stay?'

Trust his mother to cut straight to the point.

'I am.' Harper smiled, but that steely glint was back in her eye.

'Oh,' Biddie said, her eyes widening in surprise.

'Yes, MMH is very lucky to have her,' Logan added, his jaw clenched in frustration. The last thing he wanted while trying to forge a fresh start with Harper, both professionally and personally, was his parents spooking her off with some thoughtless or offhand comment. He had no idea what kind of relationship he and Harper might be able to salvage, he just knew he was struggling to ignore their chemistry and he wanted to clear the air.

'Why don't you look around,' he suggested to his parents, 'while Harper and I finish our conversation.' He stood at Harper's side, hoping his body language was clear. 'There are some very talented up-and-coming artists exhibiting. I particularly like Harper's friend Jake Barrington, so look out for his work. Might be worth an investment if you're in the market.'

'We will,' Carter said, accepting two glasses of champagne before passing one to his wife. With a final smile, they trailed off, leaving him and Harper alone once more.

'They looked *really* pleased to see me,' Harper said, glancing after them as they admired the art.

'Do you care either way?' he asked, because he'd stopped caring what his parents thought many years ago.

'*You* used to care,' she pointed out with a smirk.

Logan's jaw tightened. 'I'm not a kid any

more. I no longer need their approval. And you're no longer their daughter-in-law, so you *definitely* shouldn't care what they think.' He held her stare, his heart pounding as his regrets resurfaced. 'As far as I'm concerned, Harper, you never needed their approval,' he said quietly, because he should have protected her from his parents' expectations back then, not abandoned her to deal with them alone.

'I don't care,' she said, her chin tilted up. 'And you didn't need to defend me, you know. Like you said, we're no longer a couple, so it's not your job. I can take care of myself, same as always.'

Logan sighed, his protective urges where this woman was concerned a hard habit to break. 'I know you've always valued your independent streak. But I also know how you felt our different upbringings mattered while we were together. For the record, for me, our differences were one of the things I liked most about you.'

Her shock gave him little pleasure, his regrets coming too late to avoid the damage he'd inflicted on their relationship with his carelessness. 'You didn't care about inconsequential things,' he went on. 'You stopped me from taking myself too seriously and showed me how privileged my life was.' He raised his glass. 'So cheers to that.'

Almost reluctantly, she touched her flute to his and took a sip, peering at him over the rim with caution that made him wonder with a sinking stomach if they'd ever be able to move past their history.

'Well… I'd…um…better look for Jake. I've neglected him for too long,' she said. 'Have a good evening.' And she wandered off.

Logan watched her go, his frustration building. When he'd seen her tonight, he'd felt as if he'd been given that chance to make things right. But it seemed that Harper hadn't changed as much as she'd made out, at least when it came to her emotional guarding and holding him at arm's length. He hadn't recognised it as such when they were together, but now it was obvious. She might have kissed him with the same passion he remembered; she might have thought about him and their unfinished business, but she clearly wasn't ready to forgive him, and he needed to find some way to be okay with that.

CHAPTER SIX

'HARPER,' SOMEONE CALLED after her as she left the gallery and headed for the subway. Of course she'd know Logan's voice anywhere. Her stomach fluttered as she stopped in her tracks and turned to find him hurrying after her.

'Let me give you a ride home,' he said, catching up in three easy strides.

'There's no need. I'm fine.' The last place she needed to be was trapped in another enclosed space with him, not when he looked so casually sexy in his shirt and sports jacket and smelled divine. She was confused enough after their kiss, after seeing him unexpectedly tonight, after his admission that he'd yearned for their relationship after the divorce. Not to mention his display of possessiveness and the way he'd protected her from his parents, not that she'd needed him to, of course. She'd always been self-sufficient and he'd been right. She no longer needed the Grants' approval.

'Please,' he said, his eyes pleading. 'It's late. I know you're independent, but if you get on the subway, I'll most likely be awake half the night worrying if you made it home safely. We don't have to talk. Just let me see you home.'

Harper watched him curiously, her heart pounding with confusion. She'd never denied that Logan was a considerate and caring person. It's what made him a great doctor, but she was no longer used to him caring about *her*. His words from earlier slid through her mind.

'As far as I'm concerned, Harper, you never needed their approval.'

Was that true? Had she created an unnecessary issue because of how she'd felt about herself? Somehow defective, her self-esteem damaged because her mother had been able to desert her and never look back?

'Shouldn't you stay at the exhibition?' she asked with a shiver, wishing she'd worn pants instead of a dress, because the temperatures had dropped.

Logan shrugged. 'I've done my duty as sponsor—paid for the event, spoken to the artists, purchased a painting.'

'Okay,' she finally conceded, her stomach knotting. 'But I'm probably not heading your way. I live on East Seventh Street, near Tompkins Square Park.'

He smiled and led the way. 'I live in the Village, too.'

Harper laughed. 'Yes, most likely the West Village,' she said about the city's most expensive neighbourhood.

'What can I say…' He shrugged. 'I like beautiful things, and I work hard for them.'

'Fair enough.' Harper laughed and let it go as they walked around the corner to an underground parking garage. These days, she was more secure about herself. She'd too worked hard, had a great career she loved and earned a comfortable income. Logan had been correct earlier. Where a twenty-something Harper had tried to fit in with her in-laws and never quite made the grade, the Harper who was almost forty, didn't need their approval or anyone else's.

His comments earlier, about how he'd liked her for their differences, had almost floored her. She certainly hadn't felt confident of that at the time. Or maybe she'd been too messed up when they were together to see things clearly. Now it added to the growing sense that maybe she hadn't really known Logan at all. With every day that passed, she learned something new about him. He *was* different. Inconveniently so.

'Nice car,' she said, as she slid into the passenger seat and was instantly cocooned in the heated leather upholstery. 'I see you're still a bit of a motorhead.'

Logan smiled and stroked the dash, lovingly. 'Another beautiful thing I can't deny myself. What do you drive these days?' he asked, scanning the street for traffic and then pulling out.

'I take the subway,' she said, laughing at him once more, but he seemed to take it in good humour. 'Your parents looked…well,' she added, magnanimously. It was the least she could do after Logan's friendship and support of Charlie. 'Are they?'

'Dad had a myocardial infarction three years ago,' he said, sobering. 'He has a coronary artery stent now, and Mum has developed rheumatoid arthritis, so she's had to give up a lot of things, including her beloved golf.'

'I'm sorry. I didn't know.' So Logan, too, had to deal with ageing parents.

Logan glanced her way. 'Why would you?'

'Is Carter still working?' she asked, keeping the conversation going because otherwise she might be tempted to analyse the way he was looking at her, the way he'd been looking at her all night: with hunger. The sexual tension between them at the gallery had been off the scale, mainly because Harper had spent the past two days reliving that steamy make-out session, wondering how good it would feel if they hadn't stopped. But they'd agreed it was a stupid mistake brought on by emotional stress.

'He's semi-retired,' Logan said, driving the way he operated—with wildly attractive confidence. 'My sister took over as CEO last year.'

Logan's sister, Sarah was the youngest of the Grants' three children, and the only one who'd followed in Carter's footsteps and joined the family business. 'And Sam? What's he up to now?'

'He's a paediatric plastic and reconstructive surgeon. He's just returned from two years in Uruguay and will soon be joining us at MMH.'

'Wow... I bet your parents are happy that at least one of you took an interest in the Grant Group.'

'How's Charlie doing?' he asked, changing the subject.

'He's good. He's joined a diabetes support group. I'm sure he'll tell you all about it the next time you two meet up.' She still found the fact that her ex-husband had stayed in touch with her father baffling, unless it was part of him struggling to let go...

'I popped into MMH this morning to check on baby Alex,' he said, dragging Harper from that inconvenient thought as the lights changed and slowed to a stop. 'The occluder seems to be working. His lung function is improved. He's put on a few grams. Hopefully we can get him off the ventilator soon.'

'That's really good news. Are you feeling better about the arrest now?' She'd heard from the NICU staff that Alex's mother in particular had taken the news badly and yelled at Logan in the family room. Sometimes patients' relatives needed to express their fear out loud, not that it was easy to hear as a doctor.

He shrugged and looked straight ahead. 'I never want to acclimatise to losing patients, or almost losing them, as in this case.'

'No, but we're not dealing with healthy babies,' she pushed, because it could so easily have been her procedure. 'All of our patients are at risk. Arrhythmias are more common in babies with congenital heart defects. And if we didn't operate or intervene, most of them would have a greatly shortened life expectancy. You can't take the lashing out from a scared and emotional relative personally.'

'Thanks for saying that. I know we're not friends, but I appreciate your support, especially after...' His lips thinned. 'Well, you don't owe me any loyalty.'

He drove the final block in silence, and Harper joined him, too confused to risk further conversation. Were they forming a truce? Maybe he was right about clearing the air.

Maybe it would help them both, especially as they couldn't avoid each other.

As he pulled up outside her building, he turned off the engine and turned to face her. 'Mind if I see you inside?' he asked, that determined look he'd worn outside the gallery back in his eyes.

'What…?' she said playfully. 'You don't like my neighbourhood?'

He smiled, but his stare hardened. 'Humour me, for old time's sake,' he said, falling serious, his hand still gripping the wheel tight enough to outline his knuckles.

'Okay, sure. Thanks.' She stepped out of the car and took her keys from her bag, her stomach swooping because they might not be friends, but his considerate gestures were adding to her confusion. 'I'm on the ground floor.'

She keyed in the code to unlock the door to the street and paused in the dimly lit corridor outside her apartment, her nerves shredded. Bad enough that she'd seen him tonight, without his displays of maturity, attentiveness and honesty, which highlighted how different he seemed. The things she'd learned about him since being back had left her almost second-guessing her past memories. And he'd been right earlier: the one thing that hadn't changed in the slightest was their intense chemistry.

'Well, thanks for the lovely warm ride,' she said, trying to think of anything but that kiss and how badly she wanted to do it again. 'I didn't plan the right outfit for the subway, I guess.'

Suddenly, she struggled to breathe deeply enough as she looked up at him. Perhaps they did have unfinished business. There'd been no switch to flick to turn off her feelings after the divorce. It had taken time to fall out of love when they hadn't worked out.

'You're welcome, Harper.' His look swept over her down to her toes, and her chest tightened. 'You look amazing, but then you always did, whatever you wore.'

She froze, her body flooded with heat as she recognised the hunger that was back in his stare. Why was he doing this? Reminding her that they'd once meant the world to each other? Reminding her that those bad habits she was terrified to indulge would feel, oh, so good?

'Logan...' she groaned pleadingly, her head telling her to walk away. To enter her apartment and close the door on him. But no matter how foolish it was, she was still ensnared by their chemistry, by the changes in him, by their past connection and the knowledge that, on some level, she knew this man, who was decent and caring and incredibly sexy.

'Harper…?' he said, his glance shifting over her face and his breathing speeding up.

She parted her lips to say goodnight, to tell him to leave, but no sound emerged, only a resigned sigh she felt to the very tips of her toes.

'Go inside,' he urged, not moving a muscle. But his eyes blazed in the dim light, his voice almost an order, as if he was clinging to their last shred of sense by his fingernails.

She should obey. If she kissed him again, the way she wanted to, she wouldn't be able to stop this time. But maybe this was what they both needed, to tie up that loose end, the unfinished business, to move past their history and finally lay *them* to rest.

Her heart galloped as she stood there convincing herself, bargaining. She had no idea who moved first, but then it didn't matter. His mouth captured hers, roughly, almost reluctantly. Harper's legs trembled as his fingers tunnelled into her hair, holding her firm in that way she remembered, as if he couldn't bear the idea of their kiss ending. She moaned, parting her lips, melting into the kiss that she could no more fight than she could forget.

'Logan…' she gasped, as he trailed his mouth down the side of her neck, pressing every sensitised inch of her body hard against his. She gripped his jacket in her fists, holding him captive as his lips hit every erogenous zone on her neck.

'I know,' he groaned, shoving one thigh between her legs, parting them. The heat and firmness of him right where she craved him was incredible and made her eyes roll closed in bliss. Harper's knees buckled, her weight sagging against him, her lips seeking his once more. These kisses were way more dangerous than the ones in his office. Her bedroom was mere feet away. But she couldn't seem to find the energy to care, not when he seemed to still know her body so well, his touch lighting up her every nerve as if he remembered what she liked and how to turn her into a sobbing mess.

'Invite me in or kick me out,' he urged, his words whispered against her skin beneath her ear as his hand cupped her breast, the thumb rubbing her nipple into delicious awakening that left her gasping for breath and mentally incoherent.

Too turned-on to think, let alone speak or act in her own best interests, Harper spun in his arms and jammed her key into the lock. 'Hurry,' she said, spilling inside her darkened apartment. She didn't want to question this or think it through. She didn't have to forgive him to trust him with her body. She just wanted to feel, to relive the one thing about their relationship that had been so good, so easy. She wanted closure.

Behind her, Logan kicked the door closed and pressed his body to hers from behind, his lips once more finding that sensitive place on her neck, his hands gripping her hips, his erection pressed into her backside. 'Tell me you want this, same as me. I need to hear you say it, Harper. No more denials or pretending.'

His hot breath, his demands that she face up to wanting him, sent shivers down her spine so she groaned silently. 'I want this,' she admitted, swallowing hard.

'So do I.' He spun her around, his mouth capturing hers once more as he slid his hands under the hem of her dress, caressing her stockinged thighs and the cheeks of her backside as he ground his hard length into her belly. Harper gasped into his kiss as his fingers delved between her legs, stroking her through her underwear, zinging her body to electrifying life. This man had once known her body almost better than she had herself. He'd worshipped every inch of her with his mouth, his hands, his greedy stare and his words of love. But this wasn't about love. Just sex.

Pulling back from his kiss, she took his hand and led him across her tiny living room to the bedroom, praying that he had a condom on him, because she hadn't anticipated this. They collapsed on the bed together, lips clashing, tongues surging, hands torn between caresses and frantic tugs at each other's clothing.

It was fast and frantic, but Harper didn't want time to think in case she changed her mind. Logan paused to fish a condom from his wallet, placing it on the nightstand. Then he turned on the lamp, casting the bedroom in a golden glow.

'I want to see you,' he said, undoing the last few buttons of his shirt, revealing his muscular and hairy chest.

Harper snagged her lower lip with her teeth and watched him strip, marvelling at his mature physique and how it could possibly be any sexier than it had been ten years ago. But it was. When he was naked, he rejoined her on the bed, impatiently divesting her of her dress, her bra, her underwear as if they were blocking his view.

'I'd forgotten how sexy you are,' he said, taking one of her nipples in his mouth and making her vision swim.

Harper moaned and reached for the condom. 'I want you, now.'

'Not yet,' he said, kissing her neck, her breasts, her stomach, lower and lower.

'Logan,' she gasped as he ended between her legs. Clearly he planned to reacquaint himself with all of her. Harper bit the back of her hand to hold in her moans. She wanted to hide from the intimacy of the act, something they'd of course, done many times before. But that was then, when she'd loved him and believed she could be vulnerable with him. But as pleasure swamped her, resistance fled. He knew her body too well, quickly transporting her to a place where she was suddenly desperate to go.

Logan paused to put on the condom and kissed his way back up her body, while her hands shifted restlessly over his arms, his shoulders, his back, as if she were relearning his shape.

'You're sure?' he asked, pausing to peer down at her, braced over her on straight arms.

She nodded, gripping his biceps. Had she ever wanted him this badly? His gaze locked to hers, as if he'd waited ten years for this moment. Then he slowly pushed himself inside her.

Harper couldn't help the low moan she uttered as she closed her eyes. His observation was too intense, his possession of her body too thorough and too familiar. Her skin was covered in the scent of his cologne and the imprint of his lips. It was overwhelming.

'Kiss me,' she said, chasing his mouth with hers. She wanted oblivion not connection.

He obeyed, but not before he'd taken both

her hands, entwined her fingers with his and pressed them into the pillow beside her head, the way he used to. Harper had forgotten how good Logan was at this. How he had a way of making her feel like the only woman on earth. How he handled sex the way he handled every other aspect of his life, with drive, determination, a desire to excel. But they'd been apart for ten years. There would have been many women since her just as there'd be more after her.

Wanting to cling to that idea in order to counter the flood of familiar feelings being intimate with him again had naturally brought up, she pushed her tongue into his mouth, kissing him for all she was worth, reminding them both that this was about desire and nothing more.

He moved inside her, his kisses deep, his grip on her hands unrelenting. She wrapped her legs around him and held on as he shunted them higher and higher, observing her as if daring her to deny the waves of almost suffocating pleasure. But it was too good to hold back. She surrendered herself to it, her orgasm striking as he tore his mouth from hers and watched her shatter, kissing up her cries, moving faster until he too succumbed to the fire they generated and climaxed with a low groan, his face buried in the side of her neck.

Dazed, Harper clung to his shoulders, desperately trying not to sniff the familiar scent of his hair as the last spasm of his hard body died. Panic replaced the euphoria, her mind scattered. What had she done? Why had she ever thought that sleeping with her ex-husband was a good idea? Where was the relief, the closure? Yes, it had been as amazing as always, but now she just wanted him to leave so she could fall apart and then pull herself together in private.

As if he too was stunned and waking up to the reality of what they'd done, Logan withdrew and sat on the side of the bed, his back to her while he caught his breath. Harper tugged at the sheet, pointlessly covering her nakedness. But there was no hiding the signs of his possession, the pink heat of her cheeks and lips and neck where he'd kissed her so much he'd grazed her skin with his facial hair. She swallowed, desperate to say something, anything but knowing whatever she produced would be wrong. Better to stay silent.

Logan collected himself first, tossing her a lifeline she grabbed with both hands. 'I'd better go,' he said, reaching for his clothes from the bedroom floor.

'Okay,' she said in a croaky voice that spoke of her mounting discomfort.

He took his clothes into the bathroom. Harper sprang out of bed and quickly donned her robe.

When he emerged a few minutes later, he was fully dressed, his stare blank, as if he'd made a conscious effort to hide any trace of vulnerability left over from what they'd just done.

'Thanks for the lift home,' she said, walking towards the apartment's front door and pulling it open, sensing him behind her. She didn't want him to feel as if they needed to discuss what had just happened, in fact that was the last thing she wanted to encourage.

'I'll…um…see you Monday,' he said, scrubbing a hand through his messed-up hair as he stepped out into the lobby of her building.

'Enjoy the rest of your weekend,' she managed before she closed the door, sagged back against the wood and buried her face in her hands.

What on earth had she done? How could she have been so stupid? She'd come home again to be close to Charlie, not to start things up again with Logan. They'd ended badly the first time around for a whole host of reasons that were still very much alive. The only consolation she could cling to was that the sex had been a one-time thing, and now that it was done, they could finally move on.

CHAPTER SEVEN

THE FOLLOWING MONDAY MORNING, after spending the remainder of the weekend futilely thinking about Harper and what had transpired Saturday night, Logan entered the emergency department of MMH.

'You've admitted a baby presenting with cyanosis and a heart murmur. Emily Walsh,' he said to the triage nurse on duty. 'Where might I find her?'

'Bay twelve,' the nurse answered, and Logan quickly made his way there.

He pulled open the curtains and saw that Harper was already with the patient and her parents. Their eyes met for a second, and that reignited awareness seemed to zap between them as if they were two magnets being held apart. But now wasn't the time to talk about the foolhardy decision they'd made to sleep together again.

'Dr Grant,' Harper said, 'this is baby Emily

and her parents, Taylor and Chris. Dr Grant is a senior congenital heart surgeon here at MMH,' she told the concerned couple, who appeared to be in their late teens or early twenties, their faces pale with concern.

Logan's stomach clenched with empathy as he quickly greeted the parents and then washed his hands. 'Do you mind if I take a look at Emily, too?'

Mom and Dad nodded and Logan pulled on a face mask.

'Emily is two days old,' Harper went on, giving him a clinical summary. 'She was born at full term by vaginal delivery at home. Mom and Dad have noticed some blueness around the mouth, especially when Emily cries or is feeding, so they've brought her in today to be checked over.'

Logan nodded his thanks to Harper, and with the parents' permission examined the baby, noting her pulse, respiratory rate and the colour of her skin and the mucous membranes inside her mouth. He gently palpated her abdomen and then listened to her heart and lungs. With his examination complete, he gently passed the baby back to Mum, who dressed her and cuddled her close.

Washing his hands again, Logan glanced at Harper, seeing his clinical concerns reflected in her eyes. They were on the same wavelength. No doubt her mind was also working through the possible causes of Emily's cyanosis. Time to give this young couple some bad news, a part of their job that was never easy.

'The bluish colour around Emily's mouth is called cyanosis,' he explained quietly, his heart going out to the young couple, who weren't much older than kids themselves. 'What that means is that there's not enough oxygen in her blood. Now that can have many causes, but when we listen to Emily's heart and lungs—' he looked to Harper, who nodded in corroboration that she too had heard the heart murmur and the pulmonary oedema '—we can hear several things.'

Taylor's frown deepened as she glanced between him and Harper.

'We can hear a heart murmur,' Harper said, continuing to outline their findings and possible causes. 'That's usually a sign that the blood inside the heart is flowing in an abnormal way,' she said, her voice calm and reassuring. 'Sometimes that can mean that the heart hasn't developed properly while Emily was growing inside the womb.'

She paused and Logan nodded. 'There's also evidence,' he added, 'that there's some fluid on the lungs, which again, is a sign that something isn't quite right with Emily's heart.'

Taylor started to cry, and Chris put his arm around her shoulders.

'We'd like to organise some tests,' Harper said, passing over a box of tissues, her face full of compassion. 'Firstly a chest X-ray, and then a special ultrasound test called a cardiac ECHO and some blood tests.'

Logan allowed that to sink in, his mind working through the list of possible diagnoses, then added, 'If you agree, we'd like to admit Emily to the neonatal intensive care unit today, so we can treat her with some oxygen and other medicines to clear the fluid from her lungs while we run the tests. We'll also be able to monitor her growth and feeding. She's probably struggling to suck and tiring easily when she feeds at the moment. But we can put a small tube through her nose into her stomach that won't hurt her at all and feed her that way, because it's important that she puts on weight. Do you have any questions for either Dr Dunn or myself at this time?'

Chris frowned, clearly struggling every bit as much as Taylor. 'If the heart hasn't developed properly,' he asked, 'can you fix it?'

'Often babies born with what we call congenital heart defects, require surgery,' Logan said, glancing at Harper, whose stare was encouraging, despite their personal issues. At least at work, they were a team again. 'That's our field of speciality,' he continued. 'But we don't want to go into too much detail about surgery until we've run the tests and know exactly what we're dealing with, okay? Do you have any friends or family members that can support you? We understand that this is a worrying time.'

The couple nodded and gripped each other's hand tighter, looking even more scared. Logan kept his expression stoic, wishing he could be more comforting. But until they had some of the test results back, they could only guess at what was going on.

'We'll leave you for now, to call your family,' Harper added, 'but we'll see you again soon up on the ward. You'll also meet our residents, doctors called Jess and Greg, who are on their way here to organise the tests and admit Emily to the NICU.'

With the action plan conveyed to the ED nursing staff caring for Emily, with some diuretics prescribed to help clear her tiny lungs of excess fluid, Logan and Harper left the emergency department. Together, they headed towards the Theatre, where they had a full morning of joint surgeries scheduled.

'I hate those difficult conversations,' Harper

said, dragging in a deep breath. 'They're heart-breaking, and Emily's parents seem so young.'

'But at least they have each other.' Logan held open a door for her to pass through ahead of him, again fighting the urge to touch her. 'I didn't want to go into too much detail and overwhelm them, but we'll also need to refer them for some genetic testing to exclude chromosomal syndromes like DiGeorge and Down, although Emily's appearance wasn't obviously indicative of either of those.'

Harper's frown deepened as she glanced his way and nodded. She seemed distracted, and he could understand why. Their work sometimes came with a heavy toll, and after the weekend, after that reckless move of sleeping with her, the urge to support her, to pull her into his arms and comfort her the way he had when *they* were a couple, was scarily natural.

But he couldn't get used to that urge. They *weren't* a couple. He'd failed her once. He had no desire to relive that particular feeling of help-lessness or hurt Harper all over again. With them having to work together, neither of them needed the complication. That being said, he'd left her place Saturday as if his tail was on fire. He needed to check she was okay and explain himself.

'Time for a quick coffee before we head into

Theatre?' he asked, needing the caffeine, but also wanting to get the awkwardness over with.

'Sure,' she said, following him into the staff room, which was thankfully deserted.

Logan poured coffee into two mugs. 'Do you still take cream, no sugar?'

'Just milk please,' she said, clearly making an effort to sound *normal*. 'The Brits don't add cream to their coffee, so I had to break the habit.'

Logan handed her the coffee and they took a seat. He had to raise the elephant in the room even if she had no intention of mentioning Saturday. He knew her stubborn streak of old. 'How was the rest of your weekend,' he asked cautiously, the awkwardness they'd managed to shelve while they focussed on their patient building once more.

'Good, thanks.' She took a sip of coffee but he noticed the flush to her cheeks. 'Yours?'

Logan rested his gaze on hers, pausing to give her time to prepare. He wasn't going to simply swap pleasantries. 'I'm afraid it was not as productive as it normally would be. To say I was distracted Sunday would be an under-statement.'

Harper froze, her eyes darting back to his. 'We don't have to talk about it,' she said, nervously glancing at the door. 'It happened. End of story.'

'I think we *should* talk about it.' His pulse accelerated. He too could be stubborn. 'As it was…unexpected.'

'What is there to say?' she asked in an impatient voice. 'It's like you said—unfinished business.' She seemed so pragmatic now, but Saturday night she'd wanted him as much as he'd wanted her. He'd made sure of that.

Logan waited, his pulse flying. If only it were as simple as unfinished business. If only he'd been able to sleep with her again and then switch off his thoughts. Instead, he'd spent all weekend reliving that night and thinking about her—wondering if she was okay, contemplating calling her, desperate for this morning to come around so he could see her again.

'And now it's definitely finished?' he asked at last, his chest tight, because in theory, things would be easier if she was right and he wrong. If they could have sex and just move on. But now that they'd slept together again, he knew he'd struggle to forget how good they were together and let it go. But just because he'd struggle, didn't make it impossible. He would have to try.

'Isn't it?' she asked, her stare holding his so

he saw the merest hint of vulnerability in her beautiful brown eyes. 'I think it is for me.'

His heart sank. Perhaps she hadn't changed that much, after all. Maybe she was still emotionally guarded, at least with him, and he understood why. But sometimes, because of his regrets, he wondered if they would ever be truly over, at least for him. He didn't want to lie on his death bed suffocating under those regrets. Not that he was making any grand promises or suggesting they get back together. He hadn't made a serious commitment to a woman in ten years. He never wanted to hurt Harper or let her down again, and with her reluctance to rely on him or confide in him or to even hear him out about where they'd gone wrong, the reasons were still unresolved.

'Okay,' he said, his heart pounding. 'Thanks for being honest, at least. Unfortunately, for me, I'm not sure I'm quite there yet… You occupied my thoughts all day Sunday, no matter how hard I tried to think of something else. But I guess I'll get there, in time.'

Harper's expression grew more wary, steely glints in her eyes. 'I think it's best for us both. One time could be a blip, an error of judgement. More than that is just indulging old habits. Neither of us wants to go there. I'm not interested in relationships and obviously not with you, of all people…'

Logan winced, but he had asked for honesty. 'Neither am I, and likewise,' he said, his stomach griping. 'Of course, we're not getting back together.' He scoffed. The idea was laughable. But sadly, he feared he'd struggle to be around her all the time and not want her again.

'Obviously not,' she said, sounding inordinately relieved, as if desperate to convince herself and him.

It seemed as if they were back to pretending they were unaffected by each other once more.

Because he couldn't let it go, because he liked to win, he pushed. 'So we just pretend it didn't happen and move on?' For him, that would be no easy feat, but if that was what she wanted, he'd try, the same way he'd had to get over her after the divorce. After all, what was the alternative? That they actually sat down and talked? Made themselves vulnerable in a way they hadn't been able to when they were married? With Harper's reluctance and his fear of failing, that seemed unlikely.

She shrugged. 'I'm really only here to focus on the promotion. My work is everything to me, as is yours, I'm sure.'

'Of course,' Logan said, looking up as another staff member entered the room. 'Sam.' He stood and greeted his younger brother, who'd recently returned from Uruguay and joined the surgical team at MMH.

Sam hugged Logan and glanced at Harper. 'Harper, I heard you were back,' he said. She stood too, and Sam kissed both her cheeks, adding, 'You look fantastic.'

Harper flushed and smiled. 'So do you. You haven't changed at all.'

The three of them laughed and Logan's ribs pinched at the sense of nostalgia. With the memories of how terrifyingly good she'd felt in his arms Saturday still fresh, it was easy to imagine that the intervening ten years apart hadn't happened. Except they had. He'd taken her for granted and lost the most precious thing in his life. And she'd said it herself. She didn't owe him anything.

'So what's your situation?' Sam asked, as he filled a mug with coffee, clearly oblivious to the tension in the room. 'Are you remarried, this time to a keeper?' He flashed a playful smile at Logan, who waited on Harper's reply with bated breath. He knew she hadn't remarried, but she must have had other long-term relationships since him.

'No,' she said, shaking her head and glancing down. 'I've dated over the years, of course.' Her eyes darted to Logan's but she went on. 'But nothing serious. There was no point falling in love with an English guy when I always knew I'd want to come home.'

Logan heard the subtext she left unsaid. She'd probably held something back from her relationships with those English guys the way she'd held something back from him. Was she that changed? Or was she too stuck in the past? Was her fear of abandonment, her insistence on going it alone emotionally, still guiding her decisions, holding her back from being happy or finding love again? Maybe she didn't need love. He could relate to that. If it failed, it ripped you apart.

'What about you?' she asked his brother. 'Did you do any of that travelling you were so set upon?'

'I did.' Sam grinned. 'I spent two years in Uruguay with a medical relief organisation. In fact, I haven't been back that long myself.'

Just then Sam's pager sounded and he glanced down at the display. 'I need to go. It was great to see you Harper.'

'See you Sunday,' Logan said, reminding his brother of their squash session.

When they were alone again, Logan turned to Harper.

'What?' she said, looking up at him with a frown.

'Nothing...' Logan shrugged, curiosity getting the better of him. 'It just saddens me to think that you haven't come close to a serious relationship all these years?'

'Have you?' she countered, her stare defensive and accusing, any closeness he'd imagined Saturday, now long gone.

'No.' Maybe they were still as bad as each other... 'Clearly we're both emotionally guarded for our own reasons.'

'We've both been burned by rushing into marriage and ending up divorced,' she said defensively.

'I guess. But we both brought our issues into the marriage, too,' he added, because he couldn't seem to move on from Saturday as easily as Harper. 'You holding back was a definite theme in our relationship, too.' The comment was uttered before he'd had chance to censor it.

She looked up sharply. 'What do you mean? I'm not solely to blame for our divorce.'

'I'm not saying you were.' He didn't want them to argue again. 'I just mean there were some parts of your life you refused to discuss, even with me, your husband. Whenever I tried to talk to you about your mother, I always felt that you shut me out or that you never fully trusted me. It used to drive me crazy...'

'See,' she snapped, 'this is why what happened between us Saturday was a mistake. Now you feel as if you can say things like that, when it's none of your business any more. We're not together. We're *not* getting back together. My business, however I choose to manage it, is *my* business, Logan.'

Logan nodded but his frown deepened because her words hurt. 'You're right, it is. Just as the breakdown of *my* marriage, the biggest regret of my life, is *my* business.' He couldn't keep the cynicism from his voice. But did she think he had no feelings whatsoever? Yes, he'd made mistakes, but he wasn't the only one.

'That's not what I mean,' she hesitated, as if confused, her glance searching his.

'You can't diminish my experience because of your own, Harper. We hurt each other. We dealt with it in our own ways. And if we ever hope to reconcile our past, these are the kind of frank and honest discussions we'll need to have, in my opinion.'

Not that it seemed likely from the way she was staring at him as if he'd started speaking Mandarin. But she must know that a huge part of him, the part that always strived to be the best, would do anything to go back in time and fix them.

In that second, their pagers sounded in unison. They silenced them. It was Theatre.

'Look,' she said dismissively, tipping the last of her coffee down the sink. 'Let's just agree to put Saturday behind us and focus on work. Okay?'

'Okay,' Logan replied, placing his mug in the dishwasher. 'But before we go, let me say this. I know that you can't forgive me, because I let you down. But any time you're ready to hear my apology, any time you want to talk about us and where our relationship went wrong, I want you to know that I'm ready and willing.'

He left her gaping after him and made his way to the changing rooms, taking no satisfaction from the fact that for once, he seemed to have left her speechless.

CHAPTER EIGHT

AT THE END of that week, after diagnosing baby Emily Walsh with truncus arteriosus, or TA—a rare congenital heart defect where a single large vessel left the heart, instead of the normal two—Harper and Logan performed the complex surgery together.

'Okay. Let's reintroduce circulation,' Harper told the perfusionist in charge of the cardiopulmonary bypass machine, which had been doing the work of Emily's heart and lungs while she and Logan had completed the lengthy three-part surgery.

While the tense seconds ticked past, she glanced up at Logan, her stare meeting his over the top of their masks. She'd grown so used to seeing him opposite her while she operated. Seeking out his reassuring gaze at moments of high stress had become almost second nature. And there was no procedure more nerve-rack-

ing than restarting a patient's heart after open-
heart surgery.

As the blood filled the tiny chambers of Emily's repaired heart and the organ once more
began to beat, there was a collective sigh of relief from everyone around.

'Let's check the sutures one last time before
we close up,' Harper said, examining her and
Logan's handiwork. It was the end of a long
week, but every surgery mattered. Fortunately,
she and Logan shared a similar dedication to
their work. And as long as they didn't discuss
their personal life, their past or their recent slip-
up when they'd slept together, they could get
along perfectly well.

'Happy?' he asked, adjusting the angle of a
retractor for a better view.

Harper nodded. 'Yes, you?'

'Looks good,' he said, with a decisive nod.

Harper sited a drain in place and then turned
to Jess, who'd also been assisting. 'Would you
like to close up, Jess?'

The younger doctor nodded, accepting a for-
ceps and suture needle from the scrub nurse.

Harper supervised the closure of the peri-
cardium, the sac around the baby's heart, and
then seeing that the patient was stable and the
anaesthetist happy, she removed her gloves and

mask, her back protesting the long hours standing in Theatre.

Harper tossed her surgical gowns into the bin in the corner of the operating room. Outside the sterile zone was a row of computer terminals. Harper logged on and began to type up her operation notes into Emily's file while keeping one eye on Jess, aware of the fact she was due to meet Charlie for dinner in an hour.

Logan joined her doing the same thing at the terminal next to hers. She'd almost completed the operation notes when she sensed Logan stiffen at her side.

'What is it?' she asked, looking up. That damned intuition of hers was unavoidable. She knew Logan well enough to know when something was bothering him.

'The results of Emily's genetic testing came back.' He met her glance, fatigue obvious around his eyes. 'She does have DiGeorge syndrome.'

Harper's stomach dropped. She clicked onto a new screen and pulled up the lab result, quickly scanning the letter from the geneticist. DiGeorge syndrome was caused by a deletion of part of one of the chromosomes. Along with congenital heart disease, common issues included learning disabilities and hearing problems. The extent to which baby Emily was affected would only become apparent as she grew. But it was more worrying news for her parents.

'I'll speak to Taylor and Chris,' Logan said, perhaps picking up on Harper's emotions. 'You have a dinner date with Charlie, and the surgery ran overtime. It's almost 7.00 p.m.'

Harper glanced at the clock and hesitated, not bothering to ask how he knew about her plans with her father. She could cancel dinner, but she liked to see her dad at least once a week in person. Charlie had a propensity to downplay how he was feeling over the phone, but face to face, he couldn't hide any symptoms from Harper.

'Are you sure?' she asked Logan, gratitude bubbling up. Informing Emily's parents of a test result wasn't really a two-person job, but nor would it be an easy conversation. 'I know we've both struggled with compassion fatigue in this particular case.' Sometimes, it was hard to stay detached and remember for them it was a job.

'Of course,' he said, a small smile tugging at his mouth. 'I'm Emily's lead clinician anyway. I'll head upstairs and speak to Taylor and Chris now. I'll take Greg with me. You head off to meet Charlie and give him my love.'

Before she could thank him or say another word, he left the operating room. All week, as if keeping his word, they'd avoided discussing last Saturday. Harper had avoided Logan as best she could, seeing him often, but never straying from patient-related conversations. If she tried really hard, she could almost convince herself that that night hadn't happened. But now the phrase *Be careful what you wish for* looped through her head. She'd wanted them to put the sex behind them. She'd shut down his suggestion they talk about the past and their relationship and he'd reluctantly let it go. And she'd never been more bewildered and uncertain. This was Logan. No matter how hard she tried, she couldn't forget how it had felt to sleep with him again. And even more worrying was how she'd felt when he'd said that their divorce was his greatest regret. It was as if she'd just discovered that, once upon a time, she'd made a huge mistake but hadn't even been aware of it.

'So how is your job going?' Charlie asked as they tucked into their meals. They were regulars at their favourite restaurant, Luca's, a family-run Italian place they'd been coming to for years.

'It's going well,' she said, trying to shove Logan and his offer of an apology from her mind. 'We're busy. My resident is getting married soon, so she'll be away on her honeymoon, so I'll probably get even busier while she's away.

But you know me—I love my job.' Harper focused on her gnocchi, spearing a piece with her fork.

'How is working with Logan panning out?' Charlie asked, helping himself to some steamed vegetables, while staring at Harper's pasta longingly.

'It's fine, I think.' Harper looked up and met Charlie's eyes. 'You know, Dad, you could have told me that you two were in regular contact all these years. I wouldn't have minded.' Admittedly she might not have liked the idea at first, but she would never begrudge Charlie a friend, especially when she'd been out of the country and so far away.

'Could I?' he asked cautiously. 'You refused to discuss the split before you moved to London, so I figured you wanted nothing more to do with the guy, and I didn't want to upset you when we spoke on the phone, or during your visits home. Those were precious moments for me.'

'Me too,' she said, her eyes welling up. 'But I'm sorry if I made things awkward for you, Dad.' Harper ducked her head in shame. 'I didn't want that.' Logan was a decent man. He'd certainly been a better ex-son-in-law than she had been an ex-daughter-in-law...

'Not awkward,' Charlie said, reaching for her

hand. 'I was just worried for you, that's all. You know you'll always have my loyalty, kiddo. Never doubt that. It's just that Logan was a good son-in-law to me while you two were together.'

She nodded, her throat hot as memories flooded her mind, and Charlie continued. 'When you told me it was over, I didn't like that he'd hurt you. But after you left for London, he came to me and explained everything... After that, it seemed rude to blank the man. You know me; that's not my style.'

'Of course not. I wouldn't have wanted you to do that for my sake.' She took a sip of water, her confusion growing. 'So what did he say? About us, I mean.' Had Logan blamed Harper for their split? That seemed unlikely. Charlie wouldn't have stood by him all these years if all he'd had to say were criticisms. And Logan seemed willing to admit his part in their past mistakes. Again, it stunned her to think that while she'd been moving on in London, throwing herself into work and making new friends, Logan had been back here, stuck with his regrets. Her pulse vibrated in her fingertips. She shouldn't torture herself this way; it was in the past and irrelevant, but for some reason, she needed to know.

Charlie paused, looking uncomfortable. 'He was in a pretty bad way for a while, as I'm sure you were, too. He loved you. You'd loved each other. That was obvious to see. And it's hard to just switch off your feelings, isn't it?'

'It is…' Harper reached across the table and took his hand, knowing he was thinking about his own marriage breakdown. When Harper was old enough to understand, Charlie had once told her how Harper's mother had had an affair with a married work colleague and how they'd run off together, breaking many hearts in the process, not just hers and Charlie's.

And where Logan was concerned, falling out of love with him had been a gradual process for Harper, too. No quick fix.

'Then, in typical Logan style,' Charlie went on, 'he owned up to his mistakes. He said he'd let you down one time too many. He'd taken you for granted and thrown himself into his career. He'd allowed little things to grow into big issues instead of communicating effectively or squashing them and holding sight of what was important.'

Harper nodded, her appetite vanishing by the minute. It was only what Logan had hinted at to her, but to hear it from Charlie added extra weight somehow.

'I didn't know he felt as if he'd taken me for granted.' She had felt abandoned, lonely, a low priority. After her mother's desertion, that had cut deep, because she'd let her guard down with Logan. 'But the truth is we were both to blame for those communication issues,' she said, feeling sick. 'There was a part of me that never felt as if I fit in with his family so I withdrew instead of explaining why. I found his parents in particular suffocating and overbearing. Logan and I argued about that a lot.' Now she could see how she'd put Logan in an impossible position. You couldn't choose your family. She knew that better than anyone—otherwise she'd have chosen a mother who'd wanted a relationship with her daughter.

Charlie abandoned his cutlery and turned even more serious. 'Was I to blame for how you felt different? I tried to raise you to be confident and to know your worth, but I couldn't wholly make up for what your mother had done in abandoning you. I can forgive her for falling out of love and leaving me, but I'll never understand that.'

'No, Dad,' Harper cried, horrified. 'Absolutely not.' She gripped his hand tighter. 'You are the best father in the world. You gave me everything. If, as an adult, I allowed things to mess with my head, that's on me, not you. Maybe Logan and I rushed into marrying… Maybe if we'd been engaged for longer, we'd have worked through our individual issues together rather than apart… I don't know.' She sighed, deflated. Since sleeping with him again, she barely knew which way was up.

Maybe Logan was right—they *did* need to talk. She'd put it off because she'd wanted to focus on them being able to work together, because she was desperately trying to manage her complicated feelings for him, but maybe it *was* time she finally heard him out so they could both lay the past to rest.

'He said I held back from him emotionally,' she admitted in a small voice, 'and maybe I did. I never really liked to talk about my mother, then or now.' She met her father's saddened stare. 'To miss her, to even acknowledge how hurt I felt that she could just walk away like that seemed somehow disloyal to you, because *you* were always there for me.'

Charlie shrugged, his eyes shining. 'I'm your father. That's my job, one I love. And your feelings were valid, then *and* now. Try not to run away from them. Be the brave, intelligent mature woman you are and embrace them.'

Harper nodded. 'I love you, too, Dad.' She pushed away her cold gnocchi. 'And I'll try.' But being vulnerable with another person wasn't going to be easy, especially with Logan.

Charlie took a deep breath and caught the eye of their waitress. 'Dessert for you, I think,' he said to Harper, 'and more steamed vegetables for me.' He smiled and Harper loved him so hard, she knew that with him on her side, she could surely do anything, including face up to Logan and the mistakes of the past.

CHAPTER NINE

LATER THAT EVENING, after arriving home late from the hospital, Logan had just emerged from the shower when his apartment's buzzer sounded. Dressed only in a towel, he spoke into the intercom, addressing the building's doorman. 'Evening, Fred?'

'Good evening, Dr Grant.'

No matter how many times Logan insisted Fred use his first name, the older man was old school and preferred the formality of titles.

'I have a lovely young lady downstairs for you, sir,' Fred said. Logan could almost hear the smile in Fred's voice. 'Her name is Harper Dunn. Shall I send her up?'

Logan's pulse went nuts with excitement. Then a spike of adrenaline shot through him. Was she okay? Was something wrong with Charlie? 'Yes, thank you.'

Quickly unlocking the door to his apartment, Logan dashed back into his bedroom and hastily threw on some jeans and a T-shirt. It wasn't the right look to greet Harper in a towel, not when he was determined to act on his best behaviour. If she could forget last Saturday and move on as if it hadn't happened, he'd try his best to do the same. Even if it killed him, and it might.

As he made his way back through the apartment, he cast a critical eye around his living space, which was very masculine in taste but usually pretty neat and tidy given that he spent so much time at the hospital. He'd just made in back into the foyer when Harper appeared in the doorway.

'Are you okay?' he asked, his stare sweeping over her from head to toe as if he would unearth some clue as to why she was there at 10.00 p.m. on a Friday. 'Is it Charlie?'

Rationally, he didn't know what would make Harper come to him for support. She didn't want to talk, after all. She obviously wasn't ready to forgive him or open up. But she was there for some reason.

'No, everything is fine.' She shook her head as she stepped inside and pushed the door closed. 'Sorry to call so late. I was on my way home from dinner with Dad and I just... I couldn't face another night of not being able to sleep.'

She looked up at him, her expression troubled. She clearly had had something she wanted to say. Would they finally have the long-overdue talk?

'Come in,' he said, heading for the kitchen. 'I haven't been back from MMH that long. I just stepped out of the shower. Do you want a glass of wine?'

Now that she'd come to him for something, he didn't want to jinx it so instead acted as if it was a perfectly normal occurrence. After a tense week, both professionally and personally, he'd had to constantly battle the urge to talk to her about them. So many times this week, he'd wanted to knock on her door after work. And every time he'd stopped himself, recalling the look on her face when she'd said that sleeping with him again had been a mistake. That for her it was over. That she would never want a relationship with him of all people. It shouldn't have stung quite so badly, given he agreed with her, but there was no denying his feelings.

She shrugged, looking uncomfortable, so he poured two glasses of red and passed her one.

'Why can't you sleep?' he asked, his pulse buzzing in his ears. It was time to cut to the chase. They weren't at work. There were no patients awaiting them. The sex was out of the way. He wanted to hear what she had to say, and maybe, just maybe, they could finally be honest.

She stared at the glass of wine, twirling the stem where it sat on the kitchen counter. Then she snatched it up and took a large swallow. When her eyes met his once more, she was breathing hard, her chest rising and falling with her rapid breaths in a very distracting way.

'I can't stop thinking about what you said last week,' she whispered, as if almost scared to say the words aloud. 'That our divorce was the biggest regret of your life.'

Logan's pulse ricocheted. He let her statement settle between them, keeping very still, weighing up how best to respond. But the time for caginess had been and gone. He'd never been one for games, and she must know how much he still wanted her, despite trying his damnedest to squash it.

'It is,' he said, his blood pounding in his veins. 'I deeply regret losing you, Harper. But I thought you didn't want to talk about it, about us. I thought you wanted to put that night behind us. Pretend it hadn't happened.'

And by God, he'd tried to forget. It had been hard, especially when they'd consulted on one patient or another every day. But then he'd always known that working with Harper would be a challenge, one he'd complicated further still by sleeping with her again.

She winced and glanced down at her feet. 'I did want to do that, but... I've tried.' She looked up, her lips parted, emotions swimming in her eyes. 'And I can't forget. I don't know what's wrong with me. Maybe I've been too long without sex...'

He sucked air through his teeth at the sharp stab of jealousy under his ribs. 'I really don't want to know.'

'Or maybe it's being back in Manhattan,' she rushed on, ignoring his jealousy. 'Old memories resurfacing, or maybe it's just more unfinished business with you... I don't know,' she wailed, her stare anguished. 'I'm just so confused.'

She stepped closer and Logan curled his hands into fists to stop himself from reaching for her and dragging her into his arms, burying his face in her fragrant hair, feeling her heart beat against his.

'But I'm tired of fighting it, Logan, of tossing and turning at night. So... I thought the only sensible thing was to take you up on your offer to talk it through.'

'Okay,' he said, scared to move a muscle because the tension binding them together felt as fragile as spun sugar, one wrong move and it would crack. 'Do you want to sit down?' he choked out, tilting his head towards the darkened living room. 'I can light the fire.'

She glanced around his living space to the view beyond the large windows, which was dotted with city lights. When her gaze returned to his, he recognised the desire he saw there.

'Harper…' he said, her name filled with questions, with warning. 'You can't come here and look at me like that and not expect me to want you. You said you were done. I've let it go, as you asked. But even I have limits. I'm human, not made of stone.' What was she trying to do to him? Torture him to death? Dangle herself in front of him and then snatch away temptation just as he reached for her?

Her eyes turned stormy with fury and accusation and fire. 'And you can't say you regret losing me and not expect me to—' She broke off, panting hard.

Logan froze, holding his breath. He was about to ask her to finish that sentence, when she closed the distance between them and threw her arms around his neck, her lips clashing into his.

At the touch of her lips, Logan's mind blanked. Every word he wanted to say, every question he had, ceased to exist like popped bubbles. He no longer wanted to talk; they'd done plenty of that this week and none of it had made as much sense as this. Her, in his arms, where she felt terrifyingly at home, where she made him believe he could earn her forgiveness. He hauled her body closer and parted her lips with his, his tongue meeting hers as their kiss deepened and he forgot all of the reasons that this was a bad idea. There would be time enough for reason. If he could only show her how much he'd changed, how much he regretted the past, maybe they could repair the damage.

'Logan,' she panted, leaning back against the kitchen island as he trailed kisses along her neck and slipped his hand under her sweater to caress her breast through her bra. 'I want you.' Her hands found the waist of his jeans, her fingers tugging at the button.

He cupped her face, his stare boring into hers while his fingers worked her nipple taut. 'Do you?' he asked, panting. 'I thought I was just an old habit. A bad habit. *I* can be honest about this, Harper. No matter how much easier it would be if it was dead between us—I want *you*. I wanted you that first day you walked into my OR. I wanted you even when I knew it was stupid. I wanted you when you said for you it was finished. Don't you think you owe me the same degree of honesty?'

She blinked up at him, doubt shifting over her expression. 'I'm trying. I'm just so confused, because logic tells me this, us, is still a stupid move, but I don't care. I haven't been able to get you off my mind all week. I haven't been able to stop thinking about what you said in the staff room, the way you looked. I can't stop thinking about last Saturday, the way it felt so right in a way that nothing else ever has, but then we never had any problems with that side of our relationship, did we?'

To hear her finally admit they'd done something right, and because he could relate to every word she'd said, he groaned and kissed her again, his own desires pummelling him like blows. 'This has always made sense. I haven't stopped thinking about you, either. This week has been hell.'

He popped the button of her jeans and slipped his hand into her underwear, stroking her, kissing her, groaning when she nodded and palmed his erection. He stroked the slickness between her thighs and pressed kisses over her face, her jaw, her neck.

'I don't want to talk any more,' she said, unbuttoning his fly and shoving his jeans over his hips. 'Hurry.'

Logan shook his head. 'If we're doing this again, first I want your promise that we will talk. And soon, Harper.'

'I promise.' She nodded and because he

couldn't get close enough to her, because there were too many layers between them, he gripped her waist and sat her on the counter, one hand pushing up her sweater and the other hand popping her bra clasp so her breasts spilled free. He raised the sweater and took one nipple in his mouth and sucked.

'I've wanted you every day,' he said, inhaling the scent of her skin as he pressed kisses over her chest and breasts.

'Me too,' she sighed, impatiently shrugging off her sweater and bra and shifting restlessly in his arms.

When he captured the other nipple to lavish it with the same attention, she cried out, twisting his hair between her fingers as she held him close.

'Take this off,' she ordered tugging at his shirt. 'I want to see you.'

He obeyed, quickly dropping the T-shirt to the floor. Harper shimmied her jeans and underwear over her hips, and he tossed them aside and dropped to his knees on the kitchen tiles.

'Yes,' Harper gasped as he covered her with his mouth. She hooked her legs over his shoulders and fell back onto her elbows.

Resigned that his kitchen was officially ruined—every time he cooked in future he'd remember the way she looked right then—he looked up at her, triumph flooding his veins as she moaned his name over and over. He couldn't ever recall wanting a woman more. He already knew so much about this woman, who'd once meant everything to him. But this wasn't about for ever, just inescapable physical desire and old scores that needed settling.

Because he wanted her more than he wanted his next breath, he jerked to his feet and scooped his arms around her back, preparing to carry her to the bedroom. But she yanked his lips back to hers and kissed him deeply, shoving his jeans down.

'No condom out here,' he mumbled against her lips as she kissed him with mounting desperation and throaty little moans that drove him to distraction.

'I don't need it if you don't,' she said, kissing his chest, his neck, his jaw, while her hands grabbed his backside and urged him closer. 'On the pill.'

'Are you sure?' he asked, his resistance waning as he filled his hands with her breasts and she dropped her head back on a long sigh. They'd done this before, had sex wherever they'd found themselves. Another apartment, another time, but the memories added to the arousal he struggled to breathe against. The bedroom suddenly felt a long way away.

'Yes,' she cried, her hips bucking against his as she wrapped her legs around him and kissed him again.

'Harper,' he groaned, dragging her to the edge of the counter. She was hard enough to resist fully clothed and hostile, let alone like this, naked and begging.

'Logan,' she pleaded, biting into her lower lip.

He kissed her and pushed inside her, cupping her face to hold her gaze to his while his heart thundered away behind his ribs.

'I've missed you,' he whispered, panting against her lips between her frantic kisses, while pleasure hijacked his body and mind. 'I've missed this, us.'

He hadn't been ready to say it the night of the Reece Gallery exhibition, but now that she'd come to him, opened up and let him in, he could no longer keep the words inside. It was true. Their connection was the deepest of his life. He might be scared of its potency, scared to make another mistake with her, but the part of him that had been hurt when they'd split up, needed to admit it.

'Me too.' She nodded, her hips writhing against his so he had to close his eyes and clench his teeth against the waves of desire making him dizzy.

Because he didn't want to think of how they'd ruined what they had, how there was no going back in time to fix it, he moved inside her, marvelling at how something so familiar could be so good. How could she get to him unlike any other woman? How could he want her this way, but have no idea what it meant for the future?

With their stares still locked together, all the things he'd wanted to say these past ten years seemed to cross the distance. Maybe he didn't need to say any of it aloud. Maybe she felt it too, this clamour of unresolved feelings they owed to themselves and to each other to air.

'I'm sorry I tried to deny this.' She bit her lip, her breathing laboured as she clung to his shoulders and crossed her ankles in the small of his back.

'It's too good,' he said. 'It always was.' He crushed her close, kissed her deeply, held her as if he'd never again let her go. But just because they couldn't resist this, didn't mean she was his.

That was his last thought before her orgasm snatched one last cry from her throat. Groaning he came too, his body racked with spasms and engulfed in flames and his mind, the confusion he'd felt since she'd walked back into his life, somehow wiped clean.

CHAPTER TEN

HARPER OPENED HER eyes and blinked against the bright sunlight streaming into the room. Too much sunlight. *Her* bedroom had no window. Disoriented, she raised her head from the pillow and saw Logan, his head propped up on one bent elbow as he smiled down at her smugly.

'Good morning,' he said, gently brushing her hair back from her face as if she were…precious. 'How did you sleep?'

'Good,' she mumbled, gripping his sheet to her breasts as she sat up against the upholstered headboard. She hadn't intended to sleep over, but after having sex in the kitchen they'd showered together and then had sex again, this time slowly and lazily in his massive bed. Afterwards, she'd been so warm and satisfied that she'd snuggled into him and closed her eyes, just for a second. But now, in the cold light of day, she'd forgotten how to act around him.

'It's a little late for covering up,' he said, his

eyes full of laughter and heat that told her he was reliving every erotic moment of last night. 'I've seen it all, hundreds of times. Kissed it all, too. I'll never be able to use my kitchen again without thinking of you.' He tapped the tip of his index finger to his temple to let her know the memories were stored away. Then he winked cheekily and leaned in to capture her lips in a kiss.

Harper couldn't help her smile, breathing through the full-body shudder as she lost herself for seconds, relaxing into his kiss as images from last night flooded her brain.

'I should go,' she said when he pulled back from their kiss. 'I didn't really mean to stay the night.' She hadn't even planned to knock on his door last night. But after leaving Charlie, after her heartfelt talk with her dad, and with her head full of all the things she'd learned about Logan since coming home, her feet had just led her to him.

'No need to rush off,' he said, relaxed. 'I made you coffee.'

Harper glanced at the nightstand where a steaming mug of white coffee sat. 'Thanks.' She took a sip, feeling ridiculously self-conscious. 'So what plans do you have for the weekend?' she asked, as if they were sitting in the Theatre staff room, passing the time between surgeries.

'I'm playing squash with my brother tomorrow, and I have a charity black tie thing this evening.'

'Another of your parents' galas that you must attend?' She spoke before thinking, wincing when she heard how bitter she sounded. 'Sorry…'

'It's an Edgar Grant Foundation event. I don't think they'll be there,' he said, breezing over it. 'What about your plans for the weekend?'

Harper gently released a sigh, awash with guilt that she'd judged him so harshly but also secretly relieved that he hadn't invited her along to the charity event that night. She had no label for whatever this was that they were doing, but it was definitely about sex and not dating. She might be stupid enough to sleep with her ex-husband, but she was under no illusions that they could be more than casual. It hadn't worked the first time around for many reasons.

'I have some work to catch up on,' she said. 'I'm writing a review paper on pulmonary atresia treatment outcomes with Bill McIntyre.'

'Sounds interesting. I'd like to read that when you publish.'

Harper stared into his eyes the way she'd done thousands of times when they were a couple, her confusion returning. But no matter how weird this felt, lying in his bed on a Saturday morning, this man *wasn't* a stranger. She knew his core values, even if she was still discovering new things about him. And it was time to keep her side of the bargain.

'I've been thinking,' she said hesitantly, 'about what you said at the start of the week.' She ducked her head and stared down at the comforter, both Charlie's words and Logan's looping through her mind.

'About losing you being the biggest regret of my life?' he offered.

'Yes…that…' She looked up and nodded, still stunned by that confession, days later. 'But also about me holding back, not fully trusting you when we were together.' It was hard to look at him and admit the root of her part in their relationship breakdown at the same time, but she forced herself to keep eye contact. 'I'm sorry if that was how you saw it. It wasn't my intention to make you feel like that. I just… I guess when we were together, I was obviously still struggling with my abandonment issues. Charlie and I actually talked about it last night. He helped me to see that I was pretty messed up back then. It wasn't just you I kept out. I refused to discuss how I felt, even with Charlie. To say I was a sullen, withdrawn teenager at times, would be an understatement.'

He fell quiet, compassion in his eyes. Wordlessly, he reached for her hand and raised it to his lips, kissing her fingertips, one by one. 'It's okay, Harper. I understood it was a difficult subject for you. I tried to understand what it must have been like, but I had the opposite issue with my parents, as you know. I couldn't stop them from inserting themselves in my life. Into *our* lives, or so I thought at the time... I guess I just felt helpless with you. I wanted to be there for you, to help you through what was obviously a gaping wound, but I didn't know how. And everything I said just seemed to make it worse.'

Harper swallowed, regret a sour taste in her throat. 'You would have hated that feeling of helplessness, and I made it worse by just shutting you out. I'm sorry, Logan.'

He smiled sadly, neither denying nor confirming, but of course she was right.

'It was just that by the time I'd met you,' she went on, 'I'd spent so many years wondering what I'd done wrong to make my mother leave and how I could make her change her mind and come back, that a big part of me was sick of thinking about it. No one could have helped. I just needed to work through it on my own. I needed to realise that you can't make someone care about you or love you, no matter how fiercely you try. So it became easier to just block it out. Not to think about her. To just rely on myself and get on with things.'

'I'm sorry that she let you down so badly,' he said, squeezing her hand. 'You're an amazing woman. Strong and smart. I know it couldn't make up for what you'd lost, but for the record, *I* loved you.'

She blinked, glancing away, feeling as if she might burst into tears if he kept saying wonderful things. He'd complimented her like that in the past, but back when they'd been together she'd found it harder to believe. Now it just left her confused because it had been so long since she'd relied on him emotionally, and part of her didn't know how.

'Did you ever reach out to her the way you'd once contemplated?' he asked, keeping a hold of her hand.

She nodded her head, trying not to squirm at how foreign and intimate but also exhilarating the gesture felt. 'I did reach out to her from London. She lives in Ohio, or at least she used to. We swapped a few emails. She made some noises about coming to visit, but... I don't know, the contact kind of fizzled out.' And Harper had been devastated all over again. Too embarrassed to tell Charlie what she'd done, in case he was angry with her for being such a fool.

She shook her head and glanced at Logan, her pulse throbbing in her throat. 'I've never told anyone else that. Dad doesn't know, so please don't mention it, will you? I never want to hurt him.'

'Of course not.' He sucked in a breath and wrapped his arm around her shoulders, pressing his lips to her temple. 'I'm sorry.'

'She had another family, after me,' she whispered, the old familiar feelings of rejection hard to grapple with, even now. 'I have a half brother and sister I've never even met.'

Logan held her a little tighter, his fingers stroking her arm. 'I'm so sorry. No one deserves to be so badly let down. I hope you know that none of it was your fault.'

Harper shrugged, her insides trembling. 'I do now. I finally made my peace with it in London. I realised that by trying to force the issue, trying to orchestrate a meeting that she clearly didn't want, I was just handing over the power for her to hurt me again. I don't need her for anything. I'm fine without her, so why bother? We don't even know each other any more. And I wouldn't want to upset Charlie in any way. *He's* my family.'

Logan smiled, his stare full of understanding. He pressed a kiss to her lips. 'He's a great guy, and he's always been there for you.'

Harper nodded, smiling. 'Always. And now I'm here for him.' She ducked her head and pushed on. 'I'm sorry, Logan, for my immaturity and emotional unavailability when we were together. I guess I did push you away, and then, when I'd decided it was over, I ran away to the UK. I'm embarrassed to think I might have inadvertently acted just like my mother, running when times were tough.'

Logan shifted, cupping her face between his palms. 'You're nothing like her. You would never walk away from your own child if you had one.'

The conviction of his statement stunned her, even though it was true that she wouldn't. But how could he still know her well enough to be so certain?

Because she felt caught at the centre of an emotional hurricane and couldn't see which way was up, she leaned in and kissed him. That they knew certain things about each other was inevitable. They'd lived together. Loved each other. But it didn't change anything. This was still about sex. Harper had spent too long living without love to ever trust it again, and clearly Logan was the same. Otherwise he wouldn't be single.

'I'd like to apologise, too,' Logan said softly when he pulled back. 'I also let you down. It wasn't intentional, but I neglected you and our relationship. I threw myself into becoming the best surgeon I could be, thinking you understood, thinking it was just temporary and you would always be there. But after I lost you, I realised I'd abandoned you one time too many. I cancelled dates and missed celebrations and left you to fend for yourself with my parents at all those functions they loved. They had far too much say over my life in those days.'

Harper watched him closely, her heart fluttering wildly. If only they'd been this mature when they were together. If only they'd communicated this effectively when they were married, maybe they would still be together. What might their lives now look like if they were? Would they have a family? Would they have found some way to work together and share childcare? Would their love have grown and matured as they did?

'When I met you,' he went on, 'I too was messed up. By the age of twenty-six, I'd already let my parents down so much, I carried a lot of guilt. I was their firstborn, their eldest son. They had all these grand plans for me to take over the Grant Group, and after growing up with the legacy hanging over me like a cloud, I didn't want it. It was as if I had a whole wardrobe of someone else's clothes ready and waiting for me to just step into them. It was suffocating. But by putting my foot down and insisting on my own career, I felt as if I had even more to prove. I was so fixated on being the best doctor I could be, on proving them wrong and me right, I lost sight of other things, like how my parents' expectations were still stifling. Like how those expectations spread beyond me to us, and affected you. I failed to protect what was truly important to me.' He paused and met her stare. 'You. *Us.* I'll always regret that.'

Harper froze, a silent gasp stuck in her throat. Her regrets multiplied and added to Logan's. She'd always known that in some ways they'd both messed up their relationship, but to hear confirmation of how pointless their divorce had been was sickening.

'I understand how growing up with your life mapped out for you would be hard,' Harper whispered, choked. 'You would have hated that.' Didn't his parents know him at all? Logan was the kind of person who simply tried harder when told something was impossible. 'But I'm so glad that you stuck to your guns with your career, for the sake of all the patients you've helped over the years. You're an amazing surgeon, Logan.'

'No one wants to feel they have no say in the direction of their own life,' he admitted, his eyes shining as his stare shifted over her face. 'Which was probably why both Sam and I rebelled in our different ways.'

Harper's heart thudded. 'Was I part of your rebellion?' she quietly asked. 'It's like you said—we probably rushed into getting married. For me, I think it was because part of me wanted the perfect, white picket fence future I'd missed out on as a child whose mother hadn't wanted her.' Maybe Logan had his own reasons, too.

'I've never thought of you that way,' he said, his stare shifting over her face. 'But maybe there was some part of me that was eager to prove to my parents that I had my life all figured out. But I fancied you the minute I saw you.' He grinned and she laughed, grateful for the lighter moment. 'One of the things I liked about you right off the bat was your feistiness and how you weren't remotely impressed by the privileged life I'd grown up with.'

Harper's smile widened, but she touched his cheek. 'You needed taking down a peg or two. And I too liked that we were different. You brought out my reckless side and you still do, it seems. Otherwise I wouldn't be in your bed naked this morning.'

Logan's smile stretched smugly. 'Hey, I don't see that as a negative.' He cupped her chin and tilted her lips up to his soft, lazy kiss that tasted like forgiveness.

Harper turned into his arms and tangled her fingers in his hair, her body swamped by languorous heat. He'd been right. It felt good to lay the past to rest, finally. Maybe now they could actually enjoy working together. Hopefully once the sex had run its course, they could have another of these mature conversations and part as friends.

Just as things turned more determined, the passion of their kisses growing, Harper's phone pinged with an incoming text.

Grabbing it up from the nightstand, she saw the message was from her father.

'It's Charlie.' She sat up, frantically scanning the text while her pulse flew. Her father normally called if he wanted to chat. 'He's at the hospital.' Her blood ran cold. 'He had a hypo this morning. I have to go.'

Harper leapt out of bed and walked naked through to Logan's kitchen, where her clothes from last night were still scattered on the floor.

By the time she'd pulled on her jeans and fastened her bra, Logan had joined her, now fully dressed, that determined look back on his face. 'I'll drive you,' he said, handing over her sweater and scooping his car keys from a bowl near the door. His tone of voice brooked no argument, and she was too worried about Charlie to refuse the ride. Speed was of the essence.

Harper tugged on the sweater and slipped on her shoes, more grateful for Logan in that moment than she could possibly articulate. There was no time now to analyse why she'd come to *him* last night, no time to dissect their talk this morning, and little point pretending that she could fully keep Logan out of her life. As soon as she made sure Charlie was okay, then she could turn her attention to Logan and the consequences of what they'd done by being intimate again. She just hoped, for both their sakes, that she didn't come to regret her reckless impulse.

CHAPTER ELEVEN

LOGAN GRIPPED HARPER'S hand and marched into the emergency department of Staten Island Hospital at her side, his stomach knotted with concern. Harper was understandably worried and hadn't said much on the thirty-minute drive to hospital. Logan was just grateful that she'd allowed him to tag along. He too was concerned for Charlie, and after their renewed closeness following last night and their frank talk this morning, he absolutely wanted to be there to support Harper. He had no idea where this could go, but he wouldn't let her down if she needed him.

At the ED reception, Harper tugged her hand from his and gripped the edge of the desk, speaking to the woman behind the glass partition in a tight voice. 'I'm Harper Dunn. You have my father here. Charlie Dunn.'

The receptionist checked the computer. 'He's in bay fifteen. Through those double doors.'

Logan followed Harper, his pulse only slowing when they entered the bay and saw Charlie, pale but conscious, lying on a gurney.

'Dad,' Harper cried, going straight to her father and taking his hand. 'What happened?'

Charlie glanced at Logan, his expression surprised, then he focussed on his daughter. 'I'm not really sure,' the older man said. 'I woke up this morning feeling fine, had breakfast as usual. Then I started to feel dizzy. I'd just managed to make it to Eric's house next door when I guess I must have passed out.'

Looking more closely now, Logan saw that Charlie had a graze on his forehead and along one forearm as if he'd tried to break his fall. Like Harper, he hated feeling helpless, but at least Charlie was making sense, moving all his limbs and by the looks of it hadn't needed stitches.

'Have you seen the doctor?' Harper asked, concern turning to practicalities. She stood a little taller, clearly switching between concerned daughter mode to fellow medical professional in search of answers.

'Yes, of course,' Charlie said. 'I'm just waiting for a CT scan. Hi, Logan,' Charlie added, sheepishly. 'Thanks for coming. Sorry to cause all this fuss.'

'It's no problem, Charlie. Harper and I just

happened to be together, so we jumped in my car.'

Harper shot him a look that told him she probably didn't want her father to know they'd spent the night together, even though he'd kept his explanation vague. But how else could he explain his presence when they hadn't been at work?

'I'm going to find the doctor,' she said, turning back to Charlie.

'He's busy,' Charlie said. 'I'm fine now. Don't worry.'

Harper sighed in frustration. 'You're not fine, Dad. You're all beat up and you can't remember what happened.'

Charlie looked to Logan to back him up, but there was no way Logan was stepping into the middle of that minefield.

'Why don't *I* find the doctor?' Logan said diplomatically, his eyes going to Harper. 'You stay with your dad.'

Harper nodded gratefully, and Logan ducked out of the bay and snagged the nearest ED nurse. As Logan was no longer a family member, no one would tell him anything, but he returned with the ED resident, a young guy in his twenties who looked as if he'd been up all night.

'Ms Dunn, I'm Dr Bates,' he introduced himself to Harper.

'It's Dr Dunn, actually,' she said. 'I'm a congenital heart surgeon at MMH.'

Dr Bates nodded. 'We've decided to admit your father for observation. As you can see, he took a bump to the head so I've ordered a CT scan. He suffered a hypoglycaemic attack with loss of consciousness. Fortunately his neighbour was present to put him in the recovery position and call for an ambulance.'

Charlie listened self-consciously. Logan fought the urge to touch Harper, who'd gone into full physician mode. 'His primary care physician has been struggling to manage his diabetes,' she explained.

Dr Bates nodded. 'Yes, we've seen that from his file. I've already made a referral to our endocrine specialist here and it might be worth considering a medical alarm to be installed at home.'

'Yes, of course.' Harper flushed, probably thinking she'd let Charlie down by not thinking of that sooner. 'I'll organise that today.'

The young doctor offered her and Charlie a reassuring smile. 'The admission is really just a precaution. I don't imagine Charlie will spend more than twenty-four hours with us. And I've told him to let us know if he suffers from any headaches or nausea or blurred vision.'

'Thanks, Dr Bates. I'll stay with him.' Harper

glanced at Charlie, who was sensible enough not to argue with his daughter.

With a nod and smile for Logan, the doctor left.

Logan hesitated, uncertain what he should do. Now that Charlie was stable and in good hands, there was no reason for him to stay. He wouldn't have minded, but he doubted Harper would want him there. After all, just because they'd spent an incredible night together and had a highly cathartic conversation about their past, didn't mean they were a couple. Nor were they getting back together, even if they had been unable to fight their chemistry.

'I should leave you to it,' he said reluctantly, gripping Charlie's shoulder. 'Call me, any time, day or night, okay?'

Charlie nodded and Harper followed Logan out of the bay and out of earshot of her father. 'Thanks for the lift,' she said, clearly distracted. 'And thanks for coming in with me. I really appreciate it, Logan.'

'You can call me, too,' he said, wanting to drag her into his arms and hold her, to kiss away her concerns, but she obviously needed space and to be alone with her father. And he needed time to think about everything that had occurred over the past twenty-four hours.

'Thank you. I will.'

'What can I do to help?' he asked, that help-less feeling he detested so much, building. She didn't need him, but a part of him wanted her to rely on him the way she had last night when she'd come to his apartment. 'And don't say nothing. Let me help, please. I care about him as much as you do.'

Harper frowned, her stare flitting back to the curtained bay and her father. Then she sur-prised him by letting him in just a tiny bit more. 'Could you organise the alarm installation?' She pulled her keys from her purse and removed one, passing it over. 'This is the key to Charlie's house. I want to stay with him here, but I want the alarm installed by the time he's discharged.'

'Of course. Leave it with me.' Logan tried to steady his breathing while his heart thun-dered. This was a big step for Harper, who'd always been so self-sufficient, probably in re-sponse to her mother's rejection. After last night, after their heartfelt apologies this morn-ing, he couldn't help but see it as a marker that maybe, just maybe she might be starting to trust him outside of work. Clearing the air between them had definitely been the right call.

'Thanks, Logan,' she breathed. 'That would be amazing.'

He nodded and reached for her hand, wishing he could kiss her. 'Try not to worry too much.

He's in the right place, getting the right care and he seems fine now.'

'I guess…' she said, her teeth worrying at her lower lip.

Because he wanted to help as much as he could, he forced himself to press a kiss to her cheek and step away. 'I'll message you when the alarm is done, okay? Call me if you need anything else.'

She nodded. 'I'll keep you posted.' Then she disappeared back behind the curtains.

Logan left the hospital, the urgent call to the alarm company placed before he'd even reached his car. He'd offered them a sum they couldn't refuse for the rushed nature of the job, but if Harper wanted peace of mind, he'd make sure she got it. His next stop was the closest shopping mall. He might no longer be part of the Dunn family, but he could at least make Charlie and Harper's stay in the hospital more comfortable with everything they'd need for a night away from home: a change of clothes, toiletries, some magazines.

As he piled items into his shopping cart, it felt good to be able to help in some way. For a moment, back there in the hospital, he and Harper had felt like a proper team again, not just colleagues and exes who'd had sex again. He cared about Charlie. But more than that, he cared about Harper. Perhaps more than he should. As he headed back to the hospital to drop off the things he'd bought, he cautioned himself to be careful. Neither of them had been in a serious long-term relationship since they split up and they weren't in one now. He'd messed up once before. Hurt her and himself in the process. This time, whatever happened between them, he couldn't let her down again.

The following Monday, after a Sunday spent settling Charlie back at home after his hypoglycaemic attack, Harper met Jess on the NICU to review baby Emily, whose post-op recovery had, so far, been stable.

'Nothing to report overnight,' Jess said, bringing Harper up to speed on Emily's progress. 'She has good temperature regulation, healthy urine output and moderate weight gain, taking her up to the fiftieth percentile.'

'ECG and chest X-ray?' Harper asked, looping her stethoscope from around her neck and warming up the bell between her palms.

'Again normal, and both renal and liver function tests have normalised,' Jess added.

Harper gently listened to Emily's heart and lungs while she also palpated her peripheral pulses and abdomen. When she was happy with her examination, she removed her stethoscope.

'Good. If Dr Grant is also happy with her progress, I think we can begin to wean her off the ventilator. Can you speak to Greg and the neonatologists and make sure everyone is agreed.'

At least with Emily stable and improving there was one less concern. She'd had to shove her worries for Charlie from her mind when she arrived at work that morning, but his night in hospital had really shaken her.

Jess nodded and made a note in Emily's file. Before they left the NICU, they paused at the sinks to wash their hands.

'Dr Dunn,' Jess said, hesitantly, 'I don't know if you're aware, but Greg and I are getting married at the weekend.'

Harper smiled and nodded. 'I heard that you two were engaged from Dr Grant. Congratulations.' Mention of Logan sent her mind back to the weekend, a time of unexpected highs, when she'd spent the night in his bed, when they'd finally opened up about the past, and worrying lows with Charlie's admission to hospital. But as promised, Charlie had been discharged the following day, returning home to find the newly installed medical alarms, thanks to Logan.

Free to think about him now, her heart rate picked up. But just because they'd succumbed to their chemistry once more, just because she'd convinced herself it was harmless to sleep with him, it didn't mean anything serious. They weren't getting back together. Neither of them wanted that. And with the clinical lead position still to play for, with the interview next week, they each needed to remain focussed on work.

'I wondered if you would like to attend,' Jess continued, drawing Harper's thoughts away from Logan. 'I know it's short notice, and you don't have to if it's not convenient, but…well, Greg and I would love to see you there if you can make it.'

Slightly awkwardly, Jess pulled an envelope from the pocket of her white coat and passed it over with a shy smile.

'Thanks, Jess. Let me think about it. I'll let you know either way later today. And good luck with your preparations. Let me know if you need to leave early this week.'

As she made her way back to the surgical department, Harper opened the invitation. Jess and Greg's ceremony was being held in a rural setting overlooking the Hudson River, upstate in Westchester. Just thinking about attending brought back a rush of memories from her and Logan's wedding day. They'd opted to marry at a historic country estate in Staten Island, celebrating with an intimate party of close friends and relatives. Biddie Grant had been appalled they'd denied her the chance to host a lavish shindig at the Upper East Side's Brentwood Hotel, but for once, Harper had put her foot down.

Recalling how handsome Logan had looked in his wedding suit, she'd just let herself into her office, when there was a tap at the door and the man himself appeared. 'Hey, mind if I come in?'

'Of course.' Her stomach swooped at the sight of him, gratitude and longing catching her off guard.

Logan closed the door. 'How are you, and how's Charlie doing?' He frowned, worry in his dark eyes.

'I'm fine, a little tired,' she said. 'I didn't get much sleep at the hospital, obviously with just a chair to doze in. But Charlie seems back to his cheerful self. And his CT scan was all clear.'

'That's good news,' he sighed. 'I'm so relieved. That must have been quite the scare for you. What did the endocrinologist say?'

'They've adjusted his insulin and put him in touch with the community diabetic nurses.'

'So he'll have a bit more support.'

Harper nodded and stepped from behind her desk, making her way over to him. 'Thanks for organising the alarm installation and for the clothes and other things,' she said, her throat tight. She reached for his hand and squeezed his fingers. 'You didn't have to do that, but we both really appreciated it.' She'd been stunned when the bag of brand-new clothing and toiletries and reading material had arrived via the ward receptionist. Logan had thought of everything, including underwear and a toothbrush.

'You're welcome.' He shrugged, his stare lingering on hers. 'Your family used to be my family, so I wanted to help. Thanks for letting me.'

His reminders of what they'd once meant to each other left her desperate to step into his arms and bury her face over the thump of his heart, but she held back, still scared to rely on him emotionally, because she'd done that once before and been devastated when it was over, feeling as if she should have known better after learning from her mother. They weren't dating, they weren't simply picking up where they'd left off or getting back together. But she had no idea what it was that they were doing.

'Jess and I have just reviewed Emily Walsh,' she said. 'I think it's time to wean her off the ventilator, if you agree.'

Logan nodded. 'I'll pop in to see her before my clinic, but I'm sure that if you're happy, I will be, too.'

She shuddered. When had they started to professionally trust each other so much? It had been happening gradually since she'd come to

MMH, maybe strengthened by the fact that she'd opened up to him emotionally, too.

'Is that an invitation to Jess and Greg's wedding?' Logan asked, glancing at the open envelope on her desk.

'Yes. Are you going?' Harper hadn't yet decided to accept the invitation. The idea of watching a young couple say 'I do' made her...nervous. If Logan was there, she'd be surrounded by reminders of their wedding day and by sleeping with him again she'd complicated everything. Not to mention that with Charlie's hospitalisation she'd barely had time to think about her and Logan and the risks they were talking by revisiting that side of their relationship.

'I am,' he said, hope shining in his dark eyes. 'What about you?'

'I'm undecided.' Harper glanced down at their hands. 'It's over an hour away and I'm not sure I want to leave Charlie alone in the city.'

Logan nodded, disappointment obvious in his eyes. 'It's easy enough to come back if he needs you. And he won't be completely alone. He has his brothers, the community nurses, his neighbour. He'd probably tell you not to worry if he was here.'

'He would,' she admitted, ducking her head, 'but it's not that simple. I'm his next of kin, his only child.'

Logan nodded and pulled her close, cupping her face to raise her stare to his. 'Well, if you decide to attend, I'm driving, so you're welcome to a ride.'

'Thanks, Logan. I might take you up on that. Although, I don't know. The last time you and I were together at a wedding, it was our own. Won't it be...awkward?' By awkward, she of course meant triggering, confusing, painful. So many reminders, missed chances and regrets. She wasn't sure she could face it.

'I know what you mean,' he said, tilting up her chin so their eyes met. 'But it's not about us. It's about Jess and Greg. If you want to go, there's no need to give it any more thought than that.'

She nodded, the tension between them pulling taut. She wished she didn't have to overthink it. But since the weekend, since she'd slept with him again, she couldn't help but feel confused, second-guessing her own judgement. After all, she felt powerless against their chemistry, but Logan was still the man she'd walked away from once before. He was still the rival doctor hoping to take the job she wanted. Was she still scared to trust him fully, because he had let her down before?

'What are we doing, Logan?' she whispered as he reached for her and she stepped close. 'I swing between wanting to rip your clothes off to thinking it's a really bad idea.' A part of her had hoped this need would have died down by now, but there seemed no end in sight.

'I'm not sure what it is, either,' he admitted, cupping her cheek. 'I just know that I want you. Does it need a label?'

Harper shook her head. She wanted him as much as he wanted her, but it felt beyond reckless to keep indulging in behaviour that could only end one way. Or maybe that was its appeal? She was so confused.

'Do you want to stop?' He frowned, his eyes stormy with desire and similar confusion.

'No.' Harper shook her head, stepping into his arms until their bodies met, their hearts banging together. 'Not yet.' Maybe she *was* overthinking it. Maybe she should just enjoy it while it lasted, live for the moment, because they both knew it couldn't be for ever.

Logan dipped his head, his lips grazing hers in the barest of teases, their gusting breaths mingling. 'Me neither. I missed you this weekend, even though I saw you Friday and Saturday.'

'Me too.' Harper tugged at his waist so their bodies collided, despite the flashing danger signs in her peripheral vision. Their lips met in a desperate clash, their kiss becoming deep and passionate in a way that was most definitely not suitable for work. But she couldn't become addicted to her ex-husband. Not when it was a dead end, when they were still rivals for the same job, when they'd hurt each other in the past.

'Can you come over tonight, after work?' he asked, pressing kisses over her face.

'I can't,' she sighed, her body melting into his. 'I'm going to Staten Island to check on Charlie.'

Logan groaned, looking up from nuzzling her neck, cupping her face and brushing her lips with his. 'Then when can I see you again away from here?'

Harper hesitated, her body shifting restlessly against his. 'I don't know... I'm on call tomorrow. Maybe at the weekend, at the wedding.'

Logan groaned, kissed her determinedly and then stepped back, his breathing laboured. 'Okay. Then I'd better go. I have a packed clinic this afternoon and I can't be distracted by my gorgeous ex-wife.'

She laughed, shooing him out of the door, and he left with a cheeky wink that made her heart clench. But after he'd gone, she worried at her bottom lip with her teeth. Were they crazy? This could only end one way. She'd known that when she'd entered his building at the weekend. But she'd selfishly wanted him anyway.

Silently praying for the strength to keep whatever this was contained so they didn't wind up hurting each other again, she threw herself into work for the rest of the day.

CHAPTER TWELVE

THAT WEEKEND, FROM ACROSS the room, Logan's stare sought out Harper for what felt like the millionth time. The party around them in the cavernous stone barn with wooden beams laden with florals and twinkling lights, the dancing and the many conversations, faded to white noise as he watched her with fierce hunger and a strange ache in the centre of his chest.

She looked beautiful. She wore a simple green dress that skimmed her figure and made her dark eyes glow. Her styled hair cascaded in soft waves over one shoulder, her soft make-up accentuating her natural beauty. All day throughout Greg and Jess's ceremony and all night while they'd celebrated with a party, Logan had been forced to pretend that Harper was just his ex-wife and colleague, when, in reality, the emotions of the day had left him wanting to touch her and kiss her and hold her while they slow danced together.

But of course, today's wedding had also brought bittersweet memories of their own ceremony, where they'd promised to love each other until death. It sickened him how quickly those words he and Harper had said to each other had become meaningless. But then he'd always known that love came with conditions, and as well as being emotionally guarded with him maybe Harper had never loved Logan as deeply as Jess and Greg seemed to be in love.

Harper looked up from a conversation with one of Jess's aunts, her eyes meeting his from across the room. For a second, she froze, as if aware of the direction of his thoughts, which had been with her and only her since she'd walked into his apartment a week ago. He imagined he'd witnessed longing in her eyes, but it was hard to tell from so far away. Maybe that was just what he wanted to see, so he didn't feel so…alone. Because he ached and he was terrified.

The aunt touched Harper's arm as she spoke, before moving away. Done pretending to ignore her, Logan made his move, casually crossing the room to intercept Harper before she could become ensnared in another conversation.

'I've left you alone for as long as I can tolerate,' he said, slinging one hand in his pants pocket and feigning mild boredom as he forced himself to glance around the room, when in reality he burned for her touch. Maybe then, his conflicted feelings would settle.

'We don't want anyone, least of all our residents to think we're anything more than colleagues who can barely tolerate each other,' she said with a tight smile.

'How are you feeling after today?' he asked. Was she, like him, thinking of their own wedding, of their brief marriage and how they might have done things differently? She'd been right to hesitate about them attending this wedding together. To question what they were doing by indulging their chemistry, not that Logan had the answers, even now.

'I'm fine,' she said, finally glancing his way.

Logan caught the scent of her perfume and dragged in a breath. Then, because she seemed to be handling the emotions of the day better than him and because it had been on his mind all day, he blurted, 'Do you remember our wedding?' He winced at the vulnerability in his voice.

'Of course.' She watched him thoughtfully, a small smile curling her mouth. 'It's the only wedding I've had.' Then she looked away but continued to speak. 'I was so in love with you, I could hardly wait. I was so excited.'

Logan stared at her profile, an ache under his

ribs. He'd spent so many years scared to trust that emotion, love, that her words made him restless. His parents' love had always seemed to come with conditions. Even Harper's love had been short-lived.

'Me too,' he said. 'Best day of my life.' He'd been so hopeful. He'd found *his* person. But now that he'd lived through their divorce, he couldn't help but wonder if she really had loved him then the way he'd loved her.

Harper looked up sharply. 'Really? Even though we messed up and it didn't last?

He shrugged sadly, desperate to touch her now that they were finally having this conversation. 'Sometimes, I wonder where we'd be now if we'd stayed together.' He should drop it; no sense dwelling in the past, but he couldn't help himself so he went on. 'Do you? Think about the future? Do you still want a family one day?'

Something in the stiffness of her posture left him unsettled. Of course they'd talked about having a family of their own when they'd been together. But since then, Logan had shoved the idea of being a father to the back of his mind. Maybe Harper, too, had a change of heart.

'I don't know,' she said, looking uncomfortable. 'I'm thirty-seven. My time is running out. Given that I'm single, it's not really something I've thought a lot about recently. What about you?' She looked up expectantly, although with the physical distance between them, as far as anyone knew, they could be talking about the weather or politics.

Logan glanced down, struggling to look at her because he wanted her so much, but he also felt strangely conflicted, maybe because of the emotions the wedding had unearthed. 'I think I've pretty much given up on the idea of becoming a father. I wouldn't want to turn into my parents after all.' It was a glib comment, designed to draw a line under this conversation that he'd started and now regretted.

'We could all say that.' Harper smiled as if reassuring him, but her own fear lingered in her eyes. If she ever became a mother, she wouldn't want to be like *her* mother, but at least she had Charlie, who was a great dad, to emulate.

'Can we leave yet?' he asked with a sigh, pretending to find his shoes fascinating, now desperate for them to be alone. 'It's gone 11.00 p.m.' But at least they'd booked separate rooms at the wedding venue.

After such an emotional day, and after missing her touch all week while they'd had to make do with fleeting glimpses of each other around the hospital, all he really wanted was to slowly strip Harper and lose himself in the fire of their chemistry.

'Yes.' Harper's lips twitched as she glanced around the room. 'But not together, obviously.'

'Okay.' Logan's pulse bounded, his desire easier to manage than that restless feeling. 'You go first. I'll wait a suitably inconspicuous length of time and follow.' He looked over at her, scared by the power of his need for her. 'Your room or mine?' he asked, in a low voice, trying to smile to disguise the breath-catching urgency he felt.

'Mine,' she said with a flush. 'But wait at least twenty minutes before you follow me.'

Logan groaned silently but nodded. He should be used to playing it cool by now. All week at the hospital, he'd had to keep his feelings for her hidden and work as if he didn't ache for her. All week he'd analysed that conversation they'd had, where she'd voiced her confusion for what they were doing. She was right to be cautious. They'd been there before, tried to make a serious relationship work and failed, hurting each other in the process. Maybe this, the physical desire neither of them could deny, was all they could have of each other. The idea left him both relieved and yearning.

After Harper had hugged Jess goodnight and then discreetly slipped away from the party, Logan circled the room once more. When he came face to face with Greg, who was understandably a little merry, he shook the younger man's hand.

'Congratulations again,' he said with a genuine smile. 'I really do wish you and Jess every happiness.'

'Thank you,' Greg said. 'And thanks for coming. We both really appreciate it.' Greg glanced at his new wife, love shining from his eyes. 'I've asked all the men here this question, so now I'm asking you. I hope that's okay? Do you have any advice, man to man, for a newly married doctor?'

Logan smiled but hesitated. He wasn't sure someone who'd been married for two years over a decade ago had any right offering advice, but he felt compelled suddenly to share some wisdom, at least on how *not* to do it.

'The intensity of love changes with time,' Logan shocked himself by saying. 'For everyone. But your connection strengthens. Take time to hug each other, every day. Not just a quick hug, but a deep, holding-each-other-for-twenty-or-thirty-seconds kind of hug. Studies have proved the health benefits: stress reduction, a boost to the immune system etc. But it also releases oxytocin, the love hormone and reminds you of that connection that today, on your wedding day, seems unbreakable.'

Greg nodded, earnestly. 'Hugs. I can do that. Anything else, boss?'

Logan smiled to himself. He wondered if Greg would regret asking his attending for personal advice once they were back at MMH. 'Yes,' he said, resolved to be honest to both himself and Greg. 'If you and Jess don't do it already, learn to communicate effectively. Hold hands when you talk, even if you're having a disagreement or an argument. It helps you to remember that you're a team, not only when times are good, but also when they're hard, which is perhaps even more important.'

As his voice trailed off, regret pressed on his lungs. If only Logan had heeded his own advice in his marriage to Harper. If only he'd asked all the men present on his wedding day for words of wisdom, maybe they might have stayed married. Who knew, maybe they'd have a family of their own by now if they had.

'Thanks, Dr Grant.' Greg leaned in for a man hug and Logan shrugged, self-consciously.

'I'm heading off soon, so goodnight,' he said. 'Thanks for inviting me. Have a wonderful honeymoon and good luck with your marriage. May it be long and happy.'

With his words, ringing in his head, he left the party a short while later and wandered back to the accommodation and to Harper. He still had no answers about them, but he didn't want to live the rest of his life with regrets. He quickened his pace, shoving the doubts that day had brought up to the back of his mind.

Harper cinched the hotel's towelling robe around her waist with the belt and sat on the edge of the bed, waiting for Logan to join her. She'd been right to worry about attending a wedding with him. The day, while perfect for Jess and Greg, had been filled with emotional reminders for Harper. Throughout the ceremony, as she'd sat next to Logan while Jess and Greg had exchanged their vows, her mind had filled with the similar promises she and Logan had once made. She'd almost shed a tear, so acute were the memories. Her eyes had strayed to Logan so many times today, she was certain that their playing it cool act could be fooling no one.

But when he'd said their wedding had been the best day of his life, something at the centre of her chest had bloomed, making her wonder 'what if'.

The tap at the door sent Harper's pulse flying. Grateful that she had no more time to ruminate on their earlier conversation or answer that 'what if' question, she leapt off the bed and pulled open the door, hurriedly yanking Logan inside the room.

'What took you so long?' she said, surging up on tiptoes to press her lips to his in a desperate kiss that had been building all day, all week, since that one in her office. 'I've wanted to kiss you all day. You look so hot in this suit. Take it off.'

If she simply focussed on this desire, she could block out the confusion. Because if forced to examine it too closely, she might have to admit that it tasted suspiciously like regret. But regrets were pointless. There was no going back, and when it came to her and Logan, there was no future, either. They weren't making a commitment to each other, just exploring the passion that had always come so easily.

'I was killing time, like you said.' Logan laughed, his hands gripping her waist as he pulled her into his arms, where she wanted to be. 'And talking to Greg.'

'What about?' she asked, shoving his suit jacket over his shoulders, because she was already naked under the hotel's towelling robe after taking a shower, and he needed to catch up. 'I hope you weren't discussing work on the poor guy's wedding day,' she chided.

'Actually,' he said, draping his jacket over a chair, 'I was giving him marriage advice. He's a bit tipsy and he asked me for some pointers, man to man.' He snaked an arm around her waist and drew her close once more, chest to chest, his stare darkening with desire.

'Really?' Stunned, Harper leaned back and looked up at him, her hands sliding up and down his arms. 'What did you say?'

She was almost scared to ask and didn't really want to talk any more, not when as predicted, today had been fraught with emotions and reminders. But her curiosity won.

Logan shrugged, his intense stare latched to hers. 'Just things I wished some older and wiser man had said to me on our wedding day.' He placed his index finger under her chin and tilted her face up, brushing his lips over hers in a way that made her unable to breathe around the lump in her throat. 'The importance of communication and physical touch,' he said when he pulled back, 'that kind of thing.'

Harper swallowed, terrified to know if Logan had more regrets, especially when her own were beating at that door in her mind, the one she'd slammed shut when she'd moved to London.

'I want you,' she said instead, unable to fight the desire, in spite of those regrets.

His lips covered hers, and the endless waiting to be alone with him all week fuelled her desperation. She sagged against his hard body and met the surges of his tongue with her own, until she was trembling with need.

'This week has been torture,' he said, holding her face and sliding his lips along her jaw to her earlobe and the side of her neck. 'I didn't think it was possible to want you more after last weekend, but I thought I'd go out of my mind today, not being able to touch you and kiss you and hold your hand.'

'I know,' she said, closing her eyes and dropping her head back to give his lips better access. 'I kept forgetting myself, today. I almost touched you so many times.' Their enforced restraint had been the one thing, the only thing, that had helped her to contain her feelings. But where she wanted to speed things up, Logan slowed them down.

'When I was Greg's age,' he said, loosening the belt of her robe, allowing the garment to slide open against her sensitised skin, 'I was an idiot. I took you for granted, assumed that you would always be mine.' He glanced down at her naked body and then met her stare once more so she saw his emotions filter across his eyes.

'Logan...' she moaned, her voice pleading, for what she wasn't certain. That he'd say more. That he'd stop reminding her of their past mistakes. That he'd keep on touching her, so she could continue to pretend that this was real and going somewhere. 'It was so long ago,' she added, because a part of her needed to stay anchored in the present. There was no use imagining what might have been if they hadn't spent the past ten years apart.

'And yet here we are,' he said, his hands skimming her waist, her hips, cupping her backside and drawing her near-naked body flush to his fully clothed one. 'You're mine again, at least for tonight.' His stare searched hers, eyes alive with heat and possession as she dropped the robe to the floor.

'Yes, I am.' Because she didn't want to think beyond tonight, she wrapped her arms around his neck and kissed him, sliding her tongue against his and her fingers into his hair. He crushed her close as they stumbled towards the bed. Harper sat on the edge and pulled his shirt from the waist of his pants, unbuttoning it, exposing his toned abdomen and chest, pressing her lips to every inch of skin she revealed. Logan tossed the shirt away, kicked off his shoes and leaned over her, kissing her deeply as she collapsed back against the cool sheets.

'Logan,' she whispered when he pulled back and looked down at her, his eyes golden with desire. She held his handsome face between her palms. 'I'm sorry. I took you for granted, too.' At the time, she wasn't conscious of it, but now she saw that she'd almost set him a test. Holding him away to see how far she could push before he left her, just like her mother had done.

Logan took one of her hands and pressed a kiss, almost of forgiveness, to the centre of her palm. Then he held her hand to his chest. 'I hate that I let you down,' he choked out.

Harper shook her head, her throat tight with regret and shame and longing. 'It wasn't all your fault. We broke us together.'

With a groan of acknowledgement, his mouth covered hers once more, and Harper surrendered to the passion that was their norm, even after all these years. Logan removed the rest of his clothes and then set about kissing every inch of her body. With her skin sensitised from the brush of his lips and the scrape of his stubble, Harper did the same, kissing her way down his chest and abdomen and then taking his erection in her mouth. She moaned as his fingers tangled in her hair and he watched her pleasuring him. The power she held over him was heady, addictive, but short-lived.

He reached for her and rolled her under him, kissing her deeply, stroking her breasts and between her legs, driving her to the point of delirium. When he finally pushed inside her, they groaned together, gasping, smiling, kissing.

'I want you, Harper,' he said, moving inside

her, staring down at her so there was nowhere left to hide. 'I can't lose you from my life again.'

'Logan,' she cried, overwhelmed by feelings and a sense of nostalgia for all the good parts of them. 'I want you, too.' She meant it. Somehow, they made more sense now. This was even better than it had been before, when they were younger. As scared as she was to label them, to imagine what the future might look like, she hoped they could be a part of each other's lives now that they'd reunited.

He dipped his head and captured her nipple in his mouth. Then he reached for her hand and pressed her palm over his chest, holding it flat over the thump of his heart as his thrusts grew more determined, faster, harder, his beautiful stare watching her fall apart. They shattered together, her cries mingling with his harsh groan, his arms crushing her so hard, the air left her lungs so all she could do was hold on tight.

Afterwards, he drew the sheet over them, his body wrapped around hers from behind, their legs tangled together like the creeping ivy on the stonework outside. Lulled by the steady thump of his heart against her back, Harper's eyes wanted to drift closed. Part of her felt more content than she'd been in years, but something niggled at her mind. There was no need to panic, not when this physical part of their relationship was just temporary, when she and Logan were older and wiser and had surely learned from their past mistakes.

Logan's arm gripped her tighter, his breath hot against her ear. 'I can't help but think we could make this work this time,' he whispered. 'We've both changed so much.'

Harper's pulse became frantic. She held her breath, scared to move a muscle. She understood where he was coming from; her imagination had pictured similar scenarios. But now that he'd voiced it, the contentment she'd felt only seconds ago drained away, to be replaced by the sudden chill of doubt and confusion. Could she really trust his words and her own feelings? Or was this simply moving too fast? Even when they were in love and married, they hadn't been able to make it work, for many reasons and on both sides. They'd been apart for more years than they'd actually been a couple. Had they changed enough, and could they put all their past hurts and resentments behind them to make it work now? Was there any reason to believe that this time would be different?

'Maybe,' she replied, her voice so soft and low she wasn't certain that he'd have heard.

For a long time after Logan fell asleep, Harper lay wide awake in his arms. She was desperately trying not to panic, but she wasn't certain that she was ready to be that vulnerable again. To let him in and trust not only her judgement, which had been wrong before where Logan was concerned, but also trust that they wouldn't hurt each other again. The last time she'd fallen in love, it had failed, as she'd almost expected it would. She was older now, but had she really changed enough that she was willing to risk it and with Logan of all men?

Try as she might to find the answers, those questions, the dilemmas and doubts kept her awake for half the night.

CHAPTER THIRTEEN

THE MONDAY FOLLOWING Jess and Greg's wedding, Logan arrived on the NICU to review a three-week-old patient with Down syndrome, or Trisomy 21. He and Harper had agreed to collaborate on the baby's surgery to repair a large heart defect. Given that their residents were both away on their honeymoon, Harper was already discussing the case with the neonatal resident, Tom. Logan smiled as he joined them, his glance briefly meeting Harper's.

The thrill of excitement her presence always brought zapped through him, but after the weekend, he had more questions than answers. She'd been vague and dismissive when he'd, in the heat of the moment Saturday night, suggested that they might have a better shot at making them work second time around. She'd been quiet on the drive home, Sunday, withdrawn. She'd blamed it on her concern for Charlie, and Logan had accepted that, because he hadn't wanted to push her.

But now wasn't the time to discuss their relationship. He set aside his doubts and focussed on the clinical presentation of the patient.

'Benjamin Davies,' Tom said, 'is a three-week-old boy born at thirty-eight weeks gestation by vaginal delivery. As you're already aware, he has a large atrioventricular septal defect, which was diagnosed on the antenatal scan.'

The defect allowed blood from all four chambers of the heart to mix, and untreated, led to heart failure, lung damage and failure to thrive.

Harper handed Logan a ward tablet, displaying the baby's notes as Tom continued. 'Medical management so far has consisted of diuretics and vasodilators. Here's his most recent ECHO and cardiac catheterisation results,' Tom said, bringing up the scans on the computer in the NICU office.

'A complete defect,' Harper said, pointing out the large hole between the two sides of the heart, due to a failure of development in utero. 'Has he had a cardiac MRI?'

'That's booked for this afternoon,' Tom confirmed as Logan handed over the tablet.

'Shall we go and meet Benjamin?' Logan said to Harper, who followed him from the office.

She was quiet and thoughtful as they washed their hands, perhaps like him, already planning what would be a complex surgery.

Together, he and Harper introduced themselves to the boy's parents and then examined the baby, who had a loud heart murmur, an enlarged liver and signs of fluid on the lungs, or pulmonary oedema.

'We know you've had Benjamin's heart defect explained to you before,' Logan said to the couple, 'but we're here to review him today because the medicines can only help so much. We've held off the surgery until now to allow your little man to grow and to optimise his heart and lung function as best we can with the medicines. But the longer we leave the surgical repair, the greater the risk that the increased pressure on the lungs leads to permanent damage.'

'Dr Grant and I are keen to operate on Benjamin's heart as soon as possible,' Harper continued, 'but obviously, no surgery is risk free, so we just want you to be aware of the complications.'

Benjamin's father nodded and slipped his arm around his wife. 'The young doctors, Jess and Greg have explained all the risks to us. We simply want the best chance at a normal life for Benjamin, so we're happy to go ahead.'

'Of course,' Logan said, compassion he knew Harper would share building like a lump in his chest. 'And given the size of the hole in Benjamin's heart, surgery is the best option, because it's not going to close on its own, as sometimes happens with small defects.'

He paused, and the parents nodded. They were clearly well informed, which made his and Harper's job a little easier. He glanced over at her and continued. 'Dr Dunn and I will discuss the best type of surgery, as we'll be collaborating on the operation. When we have a plan and the results of this afternoon's MRI scan, we'll come back and explain the procedure to you both in more detail. Okay?'

The couple seemed happy, so Logan and Harper left the NICU, continuing the conversation as they walked towards the stairs.

'I prefer a two-patch closure over one,' Harper said about the defect between the two sides of Benjamin's heart, which allowed blood meant for the lungs to mix with that meant for the rest of the body. 'Is that what you'd do in this situation?'

'Yes.' He nodded and pulled open the door to the nearby stairwell. 'A two-patch closure has the advantage of fewer potential post-op complications. And we'll have to pay special attention to the atrioventricular valve repair to try and minimise post-op regurgitation.'

As the door closed behind them, Harper paused on the landing, indicating to him that she was headed upstairs, whereas he was going down. She still seemed withdrawn, but perhaps she was tired after the weekend.

'So when do you want to book the operation?' Harper asked with a frown he wanted to kiss away. 'Sometime in the next two weeks?'

Logan nodded, considering the timing, glad that they'd be doing this surgery together, because he'd come to rely on her skill and experience. 'Yes, or we could stretch it a bit further out, maybe a month. See if we can optimise the medical treatments and clear the lungs.'

Harper looked down at her feet and then met his stare, chewing at her lip. 'I might not be here if we leave it longer,' she said, catching him off guard. 'The interview for the clinical lead is on Friday. If you're appointed to the permanent post and not me, I'll have to look elsewhere for a job. My locum contract was only for four weeks.'

'Of course...' Logan's stomach swooped sickeningly, his mind racing. 'I'd almost forgotten. Why didn't you remind me?'

'I just did,' she said tightly, leaving him even more frustrated.

He'd thought they'd moved past their emotional barriers. How had it slipped his mind that Harper was only temporarily working at MMH, that they'd started off as rivals? He'd grown so used to working with her, collaborating on complex surgeries and discussing tricky cases, relying on each other's expertise and emotional support, it was hard to imagine *not* working alongside her. Because he'd blurred those lines even further by rekindling their physical relationship. By voicing his regrets for the past and indulging the fantasy that they might, this time, be able to make their partnership work. Not that Harper had raised the subject again the day after the wedding on the drive back to Manhattan. Maybe her withdrawal then had been more than a desire to get back to the city to check on Charlie. Maybe she still wasn't ready to forgive Logan.

A sense of déjà vu struck him. They'd been there before, Harper clamming up when she was upset and Logan feeling helpless and pushing for her to talk.

'Unless you get the job,' he said, playing devil's advocate, torn, because while he'd worked his entire career for the position of clinical lead and he was already acting in the role, a big part of him didn't want Harper to leave MMH. He loved working with her.

'Where would you go if not here?' he asked, his stomach rolling and his throat dry as he tried to swallow. What if he'd allowed his feelings to get the better of him the night of the wedding, when he'd suggested that they might have a future? What if Harper just wasn't feeling it? Maybe she was being cautious, holding back emotionally, the way she'd done even when they were a couple.

Harper shrugged, not quite meeting his eye. 'Manhattan Children's Hospital have a vacancy for a locum that I've applied for, just in case.'

Logan frowned, wishing they were somewhere private so he could touch her or kiss her, or sound out her feelings to see if they matched his own. 'But you'll be over-qualified for a general surgical post,' he pointed out instead, fingers of doubt creeping up his spine. Was he rushing into this again the way he had with their marriage? Was he alone developing feelings, risking being hurt again, where Harper was already withdrawing to stay safe?

She gave another shrug. 'Beggars can't be choosers. I still want to be near Charlie, so I don't want to move out of state. I'll have to do what I have to do.'

She sounded resigned. Detached. Self-sufficient, same as always. Leaving him to wonder what it would mean for him, for their relationship, if he was appointed as permanent clinical lead. Unless of course, there was no relationship.

'Of course,' Logan said, feeling sick. He couldn't withdraw his application for the position, just to ensure Harper stayed at MMH. But if he got the position over her, he would not only miss working with her, there would be a part of him that would feel as if he was letting her down all over again.

Needing to touch her, to connect the way they had at the weekend, he stepped closer and reached for her hand. 'Can we talk about this later, away from work?' He wanted to know her plans and discuss options, together, as a team. But more than that he also wanted to talk about them. Surely she felt the trust and renewed connection between them the way he did? Surely she wanted to explore it further, irrespective of if they worked together?

Harper nodded, her fingers curling around his as she gave him a small smile. 'Although with Jess away and me picking up some of her duties, I'm not sure what time I'll get out of here. But I'll message you later.' She glanced at her watch and stepped back, clearly distracted by her workload. 'I have to go. I'm due in clinic and with no resident, it's going to be an extra busy one.'

Logan too had a busy day ahead with Greg away, and with limited cover, so he let it go. 'I'll see you tonight,' he said, watching her walk away, up the stairs.

As he made his way down to the ED, the helpless feeling he detested almost as much as failure, grew. He understood that she was planning for disappointment if she wasn't appointed for the role. He'd do the same. But because of their broken trust, because he'd seen her withdraw in the past, her hesitancy made him nervous. Was he ready to put everything on the line again with Harper? After all, they'd failed at their relationship once. He didn't want to back himself into a corner. The last time he'd loved Harper he'd felt as if she wasn't quite as committed to him as he'd been to her. The last thing he wanted was to be in that horrible position again.

Later that evening, after a busy day, Harper had just emerged from the shower when her apartment's buzzer sounded.

'It's me.' Logan's voice came through the intercom, leaving her heart pounding excitedly but her stomach tight with nerves.

'Come in.' Harper unlocked the street door and pulled open the door to her apartment, willing herself to calm down. Ever since the night of the wedding, she'd relived their conversations, over and over, telling herself that maybe Logan was right, maybe they could make a go of it this time around. But every time she tried to imagine allowing herself to fall back in love with Logan, she got scared. There'd been a part of her, all those years ago, a secret, hidden part traumatised by her mother's abandonment that had wanted him to fight harder for her, but he hadn't. What if that happened again? What if the pain she experienced was bigger this time, because she couldn't run away, not when Charlie needed her to stay in Manhattan?

'Hi,' she said as he appeared, pulling him inside and closing the door.

His smile was full of relief, as if he'd been equally desperate to see her. Without speaking he stepped close, cupped her face and kissed her, slowly and thoroughly. 'I missed you.'

'Me too.' Harper sighed, gripping his arms. 'But you saw me a few hours ago.' They were clearly frantic for each other, this unstoppable passion burning out of their control.

'I know,' he said. 'But I couldn't kiss you then.' As if to prove his point, he dragged her close once more, wrapped his arms around her and pressed his lips to hers.

When they pulled back feeling shaky with longing, she wrapped her arms around his waist and rested her head against his chest. 'Do you want a glass of wine or some tea?'

He pressed a kiss to the top of her head and nodded. 'I'll have what you're having,' he said, shrugging off his coat. 'Can we talk, too?'

'Of course.' Harper made tea and sat beside him on her sofa, her stomach in knots. 'What do you want to talk about?' she asked cagily, because the weekend had left her more confused than ever.

'I feel terrible about the job,' he said, reaching for her hand. 'For some reason, I'd lost track of the fact that you're only a locum, that MMH might not employ you permanently once the position of lead clinician is filled. Probably because you're so sexy, you've scrambled my mind.' He cupped her face and swept his thumb over her cheekbone, sending shivers of delight down her spine.

'I know what you mean,' she said, glancing away from his doubt-filled stare. 'But we can't both win, Logan. We always knew that.'

She couldn't deny that with every day she spent with Logan, their connection built, stronger and stronger. She trusted him at work, implicitly. She even trusted him outside of work. But her old habits, her self-sufficiency and emotional guarding were hard to break. Being fully open with him wasn't going to happen overnight. Because they'd hurt each other before.

'There's only one clinical lead,' she went on, 'and since I've been working with you, since I've learned your surgical style and seen what an amazing doctor you are, I can't think of any reason why they wouldn't give you the permanent role. That's what I'd do, if it were down to me.'

Logan frowned, clearly troubled. 'Don't say that... I'll miss you if you leave MMH. You're an amazing surgeon, too.'

'I know I am.' She smiled, although a part of her felt irrationally close to tears. What was wrong with her? She wasn't normally this emotional. It was only a job and he was only a man.

Logan joined her in smiling but quickly sobered. 'Maybe, if they do appoint me, I could persuade the powers that be to keep you on. It would be a shame for MMH to lose a surgeon with your skills. We clearly need you. There's enough work for us both.'

'You don't have to fix it for me, Logan. I'm a big girl. Plus, the job isn't yours. Don't count me out just yet.

He smiled and nodded, then pressed his lips to hers. 'There's something else.' He paused and Harper felt herself tense. 'I wanted to invite you on a date Saturday.'

'A date?' Harper swallowed, her pulse fluttering excitedly but her stomach hollow. *A date* sounded more serious than sex, and after what he'd said the night of Jess and Greg's wedding she was terrified that this was moving too fast, that she'd get swept away by feelings because of their past relationship and find herself hurt again.

'Yes,' he said with a hopeful smile. 'My foundation is having its annual fundraising gala this weekend. I'd like you to come, as my guest? What do you say?'

Harper's breathing stilled, her insides twisting with fear. 'I don't know, Logan… That sounds lovely, but—'

'But you're not sure you're ready for a date with me,' he finished, flatly, doing his best to hide his disappointment.

Harper squeezed his hand. 'I just think we need to be careful. Maybe we should slow down a bit. The past few weeks have been intense—reuniting after so many years, working together, getting to know each other all over again, the job interview…'

Logan nodded and Harper leaned in and kissed him to lessen the sting of her words. 'Don't forget, we rushed into it last time. I'm sure neither of wants to do that again.'

'No.' He ducked his head. 'You're right. We should slow down.'

'It's not that I don't want to go on a date with you,' she rushed on, 'it's just that… I guess I'm scared.' She sagged, feeling drained.

'Me too.' Logan nodded, raising her hand to his lips. 'Neither of us expected to find ourselves here.' He didn't say *back together*, and for that Harper was so relieved.

She watched his emotions shift over his eyes as he went on. 'I'm scared that we've been here before and messed up. I'm scared that I'll hurt you or let you down again. But… I don't know, I'm more scared to walk away, at least until I've fully explored what this might be.'

Harper nodded along with his every word, her fears matching his and her hopes soaring with his. 'I don't want this to be over, either,' she said, trying to set the worst of her fears aside, because Logan deserved to know how she was feeling. 'It feels different this time. Maybe because we're both older and we know ourselves better.'

'I agree.' Logan nodded, too, hope shining from his stare. 'It's like we know what we want and what we won't tolerate. You're right. There is no rush. Maybe I got a little carried away because… I don't know. Being with you just feels so easy.'

Harper nodded and kissed him again because the threat of tears was back.

'So will you come to the gala?' he asked when she pulled away. 'No pressure. If you don't want it to be a date, it won't be. I won't pick you up, or tell you how beautiful you look or seduce you at the end of the night.'

Harper laughed and leaned into him, resting her head on his shoulder. He was wonderful sometimes, not that the reminder was particularly helpful when she was feeling so conflicted.

'No one knows we're seeing each other again,' he added, 'and I won't touch you in public, unless you want me to, that is. I'd just really like to show you some of the work my foundation does. I'm proud of it, and you were kind of the inspiration behind the idea.'

'Me?' She looked up at him, stunned.

He nodded. 'Yes. When we were together, you always teased me for the privileged lifestyle I'd grown up with. I could have simply spent my inheritance from my grandfather on fast cars, a bigger apartment, art and racehorses. But when I thought about it, I realised that I don't need those things. I wanted to give something back to the city that made my family wealthy. So I had the idea to start the foundation.' He shrugged, tailing off.

Harper gripped his face, holding his stare to hers. 'That's amazing, Logan… But don't make it harder for me to remember why I let you go before.'

He smiled sadly. 'I'm right here now.'

Because she couldn't stay away a second longer, Harper straddled his lap and kissed him, pushing him back against the sofa cushions. A date sounded harmless enough, especially now that he understood she wanted to slow things down. And how could she refuse this caring, compassionate, good guy Logan anything?

'Come to bed,' she whispered when she pulled back from their deep and passionate kiss.

'Come to my gala,' he countered, desire darkening his irises to almost black. But his hands slipped along her thighs, under her robe to her backside and he ground down her hips and pressed his erection between her legs.

'You don't play fair,' she said on a strangled moan, kissing him again. 'Okay, I'll come.'

'Brilliant.' He beamed and she couldn't help but laugh. 'Then hold tight.'

She wrapped her arms around his neck and squealed as he carried her to the bedroom. Maybe everything would be fine after all.

CHAPTER FOURTEEN

ON THE FRIDAY before the fundraising gala, Logan had just arrived in Theatre for his routine surgical list when he ducked into the staff room to grab a coffee. Finding Harper there, his heart kicked at his ribs. They'd been so busy that week with their residents away that they hadn't seen as much of each other. He'd barely spoken a personal word to her since leaving her apartment Tuesday morning after she'd agreed to attend the gala, given he'd been on call at the hospital. And that morning they'd also had their interviews for the clinical lead role.

Harper glanced up and smiled. Logan stilled, his stomach sinking when he realised that she hadn't yet been informed of the result of the interviews.

She took in the look on his face, her shoulders sagging. 'You were appointed, weren't you?'

Logan winced and stepped close, wishing he could drag her into his arms and reassure her that it would be okay, that they'd figure something out, but he didn't want to patronise her or move too fast.

'Yes,' he said, flatly. 'Didn't they call you to tell you?'

She shrugged. 'There's a message on my voice mail but I haven't had a chance to listen to it yet. I'm on call today and with Jess away, it's already turning into one of those days.'

She looked tired and a little pale and now that he'd delivered the bad news personally, wouldn't quite meet his eye.

'I'm sorry,' he said, feeling that it was somehow his fault.

'No need for that.' She smiled, but the expression didn't quite reach her eyes. 'I'm really happy for you. You deserve it. Congratulations, Logan.'

'Thank you,' he said, hating the enforced distance between them. But the competition for the role was always going to cast them as rivals. 'Look, we can't talk now, but before you go applying for a permanent post at a different hospital, let me talk to the hospital administrators. We might be able to work something out.'

She nodded and looked away, blinking rapidly as if she were close to tears. 'Don't do that,' she said, looking down and shaking her head.

'I'm a big girl. I can take care of myself. I don't need you to fix it for me.'

Logan scowled, his stomach tight. Of course she didn't need him, he just wanted her to want him the way he wanted her. 'I'm not trying to fix it, Harper. It's just that, as clinical lead, it is my responsibility to see to it that we have sufficient surgeons to meet the demands of the service. There's no reason that your locum position couldn't become substantive. All I'm saying is don't rush into anything.'

Maybe because his words matched hers from the other night, when they'd both admitted how scared they felt, she nodded but looked unconvinced. 'But I don't want to get my hopes up and then be disappointed. And, I don't know, a change of scene might be a good idea, anyway.' She held his eye contact and he sensed her slamming up another wall. 'Maybe it wouldn't be such a bad thing for us to work at different hospitals. But as you said, we can't discuss it now.'

With perfect timing, her phone rang. She pulled it from her pocket and connected the call. 'Dr Dunn speaking.'

While Logan's frustration built—he didn't particularly want to postpone their conversation, but he had no choice—he watched Harper's expression turn to alarm as she listened to the other person speak.

'What are her bloods doing?' Harper asked, her glance, when it did land on his, full of concern and urgency. She listened, pacing the room impatiently. 'Okay. Continue the broad-spectrum antibiotics and I'll come and see her as soon as I can.' With that she hung up the phone and looked up. 'Emily Walsh has a wound infection,' she said, worry dimming her eyes. 'They started antibiotics overnight, and the locum neonatologist forgot to take blood cultures first, so now we're simply guessing the causative bacteria.'

Logan frowned, his own concerns building as his mind raced. 'How is she doing?'

Harper gripped her phone, her knuckles showing. 'Not good. She has a fever and tachycardia. I know I said I'd assist you in Theatre today, but with Jess and Greg away, I think one of us should go and see her right now, before it turns into septicaemia.'

'Yes, I agree.' Logan nodded, glad they could still set aside their personal stuff when it counted. A postoperative infection was worrying in such a vulnerable neonate and the risk of life-threatening septicaemia was real. 'Do you mind going? My first patient is on their way down to Theatre from the NICU. I don't want to postpone unless I have to.'

'Of course not,' she said, already headed for the door. 'I'll keep you posted and join you in Theatre when I can.'

Logan watched her go, a sense of unease growing. Not just for their patient, baby Emily, but also when it came to Harper. He had a horrible feeling that she was holding something back. He didn't know what, but he recognised her emotional withdrawal, because they'd been there before. Was it just the fear that they were moving too fast or something else?

As he headed into surgery to scrub up, he pushed the thoughts and feelings from his mind, preparing for a long day.

The Edgar Grant Foundation annual charity gala on Saturday was a glamorous and glittering black tie affair fit for Manhattan's wealthiest socialites. Harper had been on call the night before and she'd stayed at MMH most of today, trying to stabilise Emily Walsh. That meant, as promised, Logan hadn't picked her up for their date. Instead, she'd arrived alone. A good thing because she'd needed the time to steel herself before she saw him.

She glanced around the ballroom at the Gainsborough Hotel, nerves twisting her stom-

ach. The place was packed with Manhattan's
elite, who were dressed to the nines. Harper
couldn't help but feel a little out of place, as
she always did at events like this, where the
goal was to part attendees from as much of
their eyewatering disposable income as possible in the name of a good cause. No doubt her
insecurities were made worse by the fact that,
as predicted, Logan had been appointed as the
permanent clinical lead for congenital heart surgery at MMH leaving Harper temporarily un-
employed. But the main reason she was out of
sorts, was that that afternoon, after realising
her period was a day or two late, she'd taken a
pregnancy test, and it was positive.

Her breath caught anew, the news that she
and Logan had made a baby still sinking in.
She was going to be a mother. That of course,
explained why she was so emotionally labile
and quick to tears. Why she no longer felt in
control of her own life and felt constantly confused. And she already felt fiercely protective
of their child. But Logan's words from the night
of the wedding, kept looping through her head.

*'I've pretty much given up on the idea of be-
coming a father. I wouldn't want to turn into
my parents after all.'*

Whatever his feelings were about the baby,
she would have to tell him, tonight, maybe after

the gala. Spying Logan in conversation with his parents and some other guests, her pulse fluttered. He was so handsome in his black tux, looking perfectly at home and relaxed in the company. But then, why shouldn't he be? This was his world and she'd never really belonged.

Rolling back her shoulders in preparation, Harper made her way over to him, weaving her way past lavishly decorated banquet tables and groups of people socialising and drinking champagne. As she arrived at their group, Biddie Carter's eyes widened with surprise and then swooped the length of Harper's simple black gown to her toes before bouncing back up. No doubt her ex-mother-in-law was wondering what on earth Harper was doing there, and Harper wished she knew.

'Harper,' Logan said, his eyes lighting up. 'I'm so glad you made it.' He leaned in and pressed his cheek to hers, one warm hand resting on her bare shoulder so she shuddered from his touch. Clearly Logan's mother had her own concerns about how close her son and his ex-wife really were, not that Harper cared what the Grants thought of her any longer. But their alarm was understandable. They wouldn't want Logan to make the same mistake twice.

'Hello again,' Harper greeted them with a tense smile. The last thing she needed tonight was any probing questions from her in-laws, who were no doubt as confused as Harper was about what was going on between her and Logan. Only Harper's confusion was amplified by the fact that stupidly, crazily, she'd realised when she saw that positive test that she'd fallen back in love with her ex-husband and she was terrified.

Logan introduced her to the man with her parents, who even Harper recognised as a local, world-famous billionaire. She managed a smile for the man, her trepidation building. Now that she'd seen Logan, the full force of her feelings for him squashed her lungs. She wasn't going to make it through an entire evening of making small talk with the city's wealthy. She already felt claustrophobic.

'Would you like a drink?' Logan asked, signalling for a waiter with a loaded tray of champagne flutes before she could even answer.

'I'm fine, thanks.' She understood that tonight was about having a good time while donating to charity, but she felt sick to her stomach with nerves and almost regretted that she'd come. But she'd promised Logan, and the minute those two pink lines had appeared, she knew she needed to tell him her news, as soon as she could get him alone.

Perhaps sensing something was wrong, Logan

finished up his conversation and excused himself. With his hand in the small of her back, he steered her to a quiet area beside the stage.

'What's wrong?' he asked with a frown. 'You look pale. Is it Emily?' He dropped his voice to a discreet whisper, glancing around to ensure they were out of earshot of the other guests while he enquired after their patient.

Harper shook her head. 'No, Emily's stable. I'm just tired.'

He rested his hand on her shoulder once more, his stare sympathetic.

'The on call last night was busy,' she rushed on, 'and I stayed on the NICU most of today with Emily. I'm obviously concerned.' Emily's condition, the infection was worrying, but since she'd texted Logan with an update that morning, there was nothing new to report.

Logan nodded, his hand resting on her upper arm. 'Me too. I planned to pop in and check on her tonight, after the gala, before I head home.'

Harper blinked up at him, her eyes stinging. He was such a great doctor. Would he be a good father, too, even though it wasn't a part of his plan. How would they navigate parenthood together and how would she see him all the time, interacting with their baby, and not fall deeper and deeper in love? But her feelings were dangerous. She couldn't rely on his vague and confusing words whispered in the dark the night of the wedding. She and Logan had been in love before, committed, married, and it still hadn't worked out. As always, Harper could only truly, one hundred percent, rely on herself. And unlike when they were a couple, now there was a child to consider. She needed to protect not only her own heart, but also to protect the baby, because she didn't want her child to grow up without knowing one parent the way she had.

With a lurch of her heart, she realised the precariousness of her situation. Ten years ago she'd had to fall out of love with him, because it hadn't worked out, a feat that had been harder than she could ever have imagined when she'd left him. And now, here she was again. Desperate to avoid the rejection that would come if they tried and failed to have a relationship, but this time, she would be unable to run away from it all. She'd have to see him, to share their child with him. The pain would be so much worse.

'What is it, Harper? You're worrying me,' he said frowning.

'I need to tell you something,' she said, her stare flicking over his shoulder, where she spied Logan's mother covertly watching them talk. She hated to do this here and now, but she had no choice.

'Okay,' he said looking a little distracted. No

doubt he had guests to greet and official duties. Her timing was terrible. But surely he would want to know as soon as possible, and now that she'd faced him, here of all places, she couldn't wait to leave and fall apart in private.

'I'm pregnant,' she said, blinking up at him.

He frowned, clearly shocked and confused, so she rushed on. 'I know now isn't the best time to tell you this. I was going to wait until the end of the night. But I don't think I can stay after all.'

His frown deepened. 'I… I don't know what to say. Are you certain? It can't be very far along… It's only been a few weeks.'

Harper nodded, feeling sick. 'I took a test this afternoon, and yes, obviously it's very early. But it's okay, Logan. You can be as involved as you want. I'll be fine doing this alone. I just wanted you to know.'

'I'm stunned.' His hands gripped her upper arms and he drew her close, his lips pressed to her forehead. 'But I guess I shouldn't be.'

Harper closed her eyes and breathed in the scent of him, imagining for a moment that the three of them, him, her and the baby, could be a proper family. But she'd learned long ago, waiting for her own mother to come back for her, that wishes never came true. Time to put on her big girl pants once more and be strong, for their child.

'How are you feeling?' he asked, pulling back to look down at her, his eyes understandably full of questions.

'Tired. Sick. The usual.' Harper glanced over at her former in-laws. Biddie Grant looked like she'd swallowed something bitter. But of course they were probably thinking Harper and Logan were getting back together and were rightly horrified.

'I can't believe this,' he said, his hesitant smile breaking her heart.

'I know you didn't want to be a father—'

'Only because I'd never met the right woman,' he interjected, 'and I was worried that I might be overbearing and emotionally cold like my own parents. But this...this changes everything.'

'Not really...' Harper dragged in a deep breath as tiny flickers of hope built in her chest, but just like she had as a child and the last time she'd loved this man, she did her best to extinguish them.

Logan looked confused. 'What do you mean?'

Harper stepped back out of his arms. She didn't want to make a scene or cause gossip. 'I mean, obviously *my* life is about to change, but yours only has to if you want it to.'

'Of course I want it to,' he said, his expression mildly hurt. 'You won't be doing this alone. I'm going to be a father to my own child, Harper, and we'll be together, raising him or her. We can be a couple again. It makes sense.'

Harper shook her head, too scared to trust his words. 'Is that the best idea?' He wasn't in love with her, he just wanted her in his life. She didn't want to be a couple only because they'd made a baby together. Not when *she'd* stupidly fallen back in love with Logan. She would die inside, knowing that he didn't love her back, that there was probably something unlovable about her after all. She was better off alone, as she'd always been.

'What do you mean?' he asked with a scowl. 'You don't want me?'

Forcing herself to think about the baby's needs and not her own, she raised her chin. 'I think we've inadvertently rushed into this again, Logan. That's what I was scared of. I think it's best for all of us if you and I focus on being the best parents we can be. We both want that, right?'

She knew this man. He liked to excel at everything he did. He wouldn't tolerate any hint of failure when it came to fatherhood.

'Of course I want to be the best father I can be, that goes without saying.'

Harper rushed on. 'So we have to put the baby first and find a way to be there for our child. Because we tried to be a couple before and it didn't work out. So I think it's best if we put us aside now. After all, we have something more important to focus on—our baby.'

'But what about us?' His stare darkened. She was hurting him again, but she needed to be strong so she didn't get hurt herself, only worse because she loved him, desperately and even more deeply than before. 'I thought you'd started to forgive me?' he said. 'Is this because of the job?'

'Of course it's not about the job.' Harper shook her head, her heart cracking open a little more. She didn't care one hoot for the job. At the age of thirty-seven, she'd be considered a geriatric mother. She wanted to do everything in her power to ensure her baby was healthy. 'I just don't want us to hurt each other again,' she said, pleadingly, 'like we did before. And if it goes wrong again, we will hurt each other, Logan. We'll turn into two people who resent each other and can't be in the same room as each other, with their child caught in the middle. I don't want that for our baby. I want what you said at the wedding. You and I a part of each other's lives, especially now, for the sake of the baby. I want us to be civilised and mature and respectful. Isn't that what you want too? Isn't that more important?'

He nodded, his mouth turned down but his stare hardening. 'Of course it's important. I'll always be there for you and our child.'

Harper nodded, relieved and devastated at the same time. She tried to smile, her eyes stinging with unshed tears. She'd been right to protect herself. Last time they'd split up, a secret part of her had wanted Logan to fight for her, but he hadn't. And now history was repeating itself, only this time, all that mattered was that he kept his promise to their child. Her heart would heal.

'That's all I want,' she whispered, her throat aching. 'Because I've been that child, Logan, abandoned by a parent and wondering what I did wrong or if there was something wrong with me. I never want *our* child to go through that.'

'It won't,' he said, glancing up and gesturing impatiently to someone who obviously needed his attention.

'I'm going to go,' she said, relieved to have a genuine excuse to sneak out. 'You have host commitments, and I'm not really in a party kind of place.' Bravely, she surged onto her tiptoes and pressed a kiss to his cheek, trying not to inhale the scent of him. 'Have a good evening and we'll talk again soon.'

Clearly frustrated, he clenched his jaw and

nodded once. Harper left the ballroom the way she'd entered, her head held high. She couldn't have everything she wanted, but she didn't need it all. She'd have a cordial relationship with Logan, but their child would have two parents and as much love as it needed. That would be enough for Harper.

CHAPTER FIFTEEN

WITH HIS HOST duties almost over for the evening, Logan checked his watch for what felt like the millionth time, counting down the minutes until he too could leave the Gainsborough Hotel and chase after Harper. Fear and nausea tussled for dominance inside him. He couldn't quite believe how she'd dropped the bombshell about the baby, killed their relationship and then run. And he'd simply let her leave...

A hand landed on his shoulder, making him start. He looked up to see his brother, Sam, grinning at him.

'Congratulations on a great night,' Sam said. 'I hope you've successfully filled the foundation's coffers for another year.'

Logan nodded distractedly, the success of the evening the last thing on his mind. All he could think about was how Harper was having his child, but didn't want to be with him. She clearly had no feelings for him. She was still

keeping him out emotionally. Whereas he…
he'd let down his guard and started to see their
future together.

'What's wrong?' Sam asked, as if sensing his
older brother's turmoil.

Logan swallowed and rubbed a hand over
his face, debating how much to tell Sam. He
didn't want news of the baby getting back to
his parents, not until he'd figured out a way to
convince Harper to give them another chance
and was ready to tell them they were going to
be grandparents himself.

'This is just between me and you, but Harper
is pregnant. I'm going to have a baby,' he said,
reliving how stunned he'd been by her news.
She'd said she was taking the pill, so he'd assumed a pregnancy was unlikely. But with time
to get used to the idea, his mind had filled with
happy family images—him, Harper and their
child together, a dream he could never have
imagined when she'd first come back into his
life.

Then she'd dealt the fatal blow and declared
she didn't want the future he saw so clearly. She
didn't want *him*.

'Wow!' Sam said, his eyes wide with shock.
'I didn't even know you two were back together.
Double congratulations.' He hugged Logan,

who winced and shook his head, weighed down by defeat.

'We're not back together.'

'Oh… I see.' Sam's excitement dimmed. He looked as confused as Logan felt. 'So…how do you feel? About the baby?'

'I'm excited, of course,' Logan said automatically. He still couldn't quite believe the wonderful news. Then he swallowed hard, because his other feelings of devastation and failure that he and Harper weren't going to try and be together were overwhelming his joy. 'Obviously I'm a bit worried that I'm too old to be a dad,' he went on, needing to fill the silence with words so he couldn't hear Harper's rejection again and again. 'That I'll mess it up or get it wrong, but apart from that, I can't wait.'

Sam frowned, looking concerned. 'Why would you mess it up? You've never in your life messed anything up. You're such an overachiever.'

Logan snorted a mirthless laugh. 'Except when it comes to Harper.' He'd messed that up. Twice. That's why he let her leave earlier. Having lost her before, he knew she'd been right: it was better to have some part of her in his life, than have none of her at all. And he would never tolerate being absent from his child's life.

'So if you feel that way about her, why can't

you make a go of it?' Sam asked hesitantly. 'Especially now you two are having a kid together.'

Of course Sam would ask the million-dollar question.

Logan shrugged, wishing he had the answer. 'Because she doesn't want to.' She didn't want him. She'd convinced herself they couldn't work and hadn't even given him a chance. She'd pushed him away again.

'I'm sorry,' Sam said, shaking his head sadly. 'I still don't really understand where you two went wrong. You're so perfect for each other, and neither of you ever found anyone else to come close to what you had together.'

Logan's stomach rolled with helplessness. 'What can I say? Last time we were both a bit messed up, and this time... I guess we're both scared that history will repeat itself.'

Sam stayed silent for a few seconds, then said, 'Exactly how scared are you?'

Logan looked up sharply. 'What do you mean?'

'I mean how scared are you?' Sam pushed in that way a younger brother could. 'Are you scared enough to just walk away from her again? Or do you want to be with this woman? Because it seems to me that you're still crazy for each other. The minute she comes back to

Manhattan, you both pick up where you left off and make a baby together.'

'I'm not walking away.' Logan gritted his teeth. He wasn't letting Harper go, not this time. 'But I can't make her want me if she doesn't.'

His skin began to crawl. Forced to analyse exactly what she'd said earlier, a greater sense of clarity developed. Harper had been the one to push him away. *Again.* And he'd allowed it out of some kind of fear to fail. He'd meekly accepted her depressing solution for them to abandon what they'd rediscovered with each other since she'd returned to Manhattan and set it aside to focus on being parents. But what he really wanted to do was fight for them. To fight for her, the only woman he'd ever loved.

He dropped his head into his hand and breathed through the panic flooding his body with adrenaline. Had he failed her again because he too was scared? He didn't want to hurt her again. He didn't want to let her down. He certainly never wanted to let down their child. But Sam was right—that fear wasn't a good enough reason to stop him from fighting for Harper, the way he should have done the last time she tried to make him leave her. Why couldn't he have everything he wanted? A relationship with Harper *and* his baby. The three of them could be a family, but only if he could convince Harper that what they had was worth being terrified for, worth fighting for. He loved her. He'd never stopped. It wasn't over until he'd told her that and showed her what they might have in the future.

Logan gripped his brother's shoulder, fierce urgency in control of his nervous system. 'Can you do me a favour? Can you stand in for me? Shake hands and thank people for coming as they leave?'

'Of course,' Sam said. 'I take it you're going to Harper's place?'

'I am.' Logan nodded. 'I'm not giving up on us this time. I'm not going to let her push me away.'

'Then get out of here,' Sam said with an encouraging smile.

Logan sneaked out the back and jumped into his car.

Needing to flee the city, to outrun her confusion and pain and to think straight, Harper had gone home to Charlie's place in Staten Island after she'd left Logan's gala. As she'd known he wouldn't, Charlie hadn't asked any questions when he'd found her on his doorstep. He'd taken one look at her expression and tucked her into her childhood bed with a mug of hot chocolate and told her that he loved her. Of course, she'd

cried half the night. But when she'd opened her
eyes in the morning, she'd pulled herself together, dressed and taken Charlie out for breakfast at their favourite diner, followed by a walk
along South Beach in the sun.

'I didn't push you last night, but you're still
quiet today,' Charlie said as they walked side
by side. 'Do you want to talk about it with your
old man?'

Harper tried to put on a brave face, to smile
reassuringly, but her heart was too sore. She
hadn't anticipated that ending things with
Logan would hurt this much. She'd done it to
protect herself and the baby from possible pain.
But somehow, she'd ended up back there, in
love with Logan and alone again. She dragged
in some deep breaths and prayed that this feeling of desolation would pass quickly this time.
After all, she'd got over him once before, she
could do it again. She'd have to, for the baby's
sake.

'I'm okay,' she said, plucking up the courage
to tell Charlie her news. 'I actually have something to tell you. It's very early days, so don't
get too excited just yet, but I'm pregnant, Dad.
You're going to be a grandpa.'

Charlie stopped walking and pulled Harper
into a hug, saying nothing. Her throat burned
as she clung to him, sucked in the reassuring

scent of the cologne he'd always worn and the clean linen smell of his sweater, somehow more overcome by his steady, silent approval than if he'd praised her to the heavens. But then Charlie had always been her port in the storm.

'Well, fancy that,' he said, smiling broadly as he brushed her windblown hair back from her face the way he had a thousand times when she was a little girl. 'A grandpa. I like the sound of that.'

'Me too.' Harper laughed, brushing away the tears that had escaped as they resumed their stroll. But the moment of peace was short-lived.

'Is it Logan's baby, too?' he asked keeping his eyes straight ahead.

'Yes,' she said with a sigh, not bothering to deny it. 'How did you know?' Had Logan told him? No. He wouldn't do that.

Charlie shrugged, turning wise eyes on his daughter. 'I know you both quite well. He actually called last night after you'd gone to bed, looking for you. It was late and I didn't want to wake you.'

Harper paused again. 'He did?' What did he want? Just to check up on her probably. She'd need to get used to seeing him and speaking to him without touching him, kissing him, or throwing herself into his arms and begging him to love her.

Charlie nodded, looking out to sea. 'He didn't tell me about the baby, of course, but I knew from the tone of his voice that something was up. So are you two getting back together? Is that it?'

Harper sighed, the nausea returning, even though it was too early to be due to morning sickness. 'I don't think so, Dad. It's too risky. There's too much history between us, and now that there's a baby to think about, we can't afford to mess up our relationship again. I'd rather he was in my life, mine and the baby's, than not. So we have to make the best of the situation.'

It sounded sensible enough, but her reassuring words didn't seem to have any impact on the ache in her chest, which only throbbed harder.

'The best of the situation…?' Charlie asked, sounding disappointed with her. 'Of course you want him in your life, but what's stopping the two of you from making a real go of it? For keeps this time.'

Harper looked away, the horizon blurring out of focus as she tried to hold herself together and not sob. 'So many things,' she admitted, hoping that eventually, with each time she spoke the words aloud, they would start to come true. 'It didn't work out for us last time, for one. We hurt each other. There's nothing to say that this time would be any different.'

Charlie nodded, considering her argument in his quiet way. 'But you've both changed. You're older now. And you are going to have a baby together. If ever there was a reason to make something work, that's it, right there.'

She smiled sadly at her dad. 'That's not enough of a reason to keep two people together. You know that, better than anyone. I don't want him to just be with me because of our child. I'm better off alone.'

'Are you really?' Charlie observed her sadly. 'You can't compare our situations. Don't forget that your mother fell out of love with me, whereas I don't think Logan ever stopped loving you, even after the divorce.'

Harper swallowed hard, fighting tears. 'I think you're wrong there, Dad. He hasn't said he's in love with me.' But why would Charlie say that if he didn't believe it to be true?

'Am I?' Charlie said, patiently staring like she was a little girl with tricky maths problem he knew she'd be able to figure out as long as she believed in herself. 'Are you sure about that, kiddo? He might not have said the words but I know him.'

Harper opened her mouth to reply and then closed it again, completely lost for words. She knew Logan, too. She knew he hated to fail. She knew he would be scared to hurt her or let her down again. She knew she too had been scared, terrified, so she'd shut down her heart to keep herself safe. Could Logan love her the way she loved him? Was it possible that she'd pushed him away again out of fear that no one could love her?

'I've seen you two together,' Charlie went on, 'both then and now, and if I was a betting man, I'd say he's head over heels. And your face is telling me that you're the same for him.'

Harper ducked her head, trying not to cry. 'I don't know how he feels...' she said in a quiet voice. Not that she'd given him a chance to tell her. She'd sprung her news on him at a charity function he was hosting, told him she didn't want to be in a relationship with him, even though that was a lie and then fled, just like the last time. Had she been testing him again? Sabotaging what they'd had before she'd let him too close, before she could get hurt or abandoned once more?

'Maybe he's scared, too,' Charlie said. 'Scared to tell you how he feels in case you can't love him back. He once told me that he'd been brought up in a house where love felt conditional. Maybe he doesn't feel worthy of your love, having blamed himself for letting you down once before.'

Harper stared at her father, willing his words to be untrue. If Logan loved her but was scared, that would mean that she'd pushed away the very thing she wanted: a second chance at loving him. She loved him, harder than before, and if he could ever love her again one day, she would grab him with both hands and hold on tight and never let him go.

'What did you tell him?' she asked urgently, 'last night when he called?' She stepped close to Charlie, stopping just short of gripping his arms and demanding an answer.

'I told him you were asleep in your old bed. Why?'

'I need to go to him. I need to find out if what you said is true.' With icy panic in her veins, Harper turned and headed back towards Charlie's car, praying it wasn't too late.

CHAPTER SIXTEEN

THE MINUTE LOGAN spied Charlie's car pulling into the street, he stepped from his own vehicle, sheepishly scanning the neighbour's house, because he'd banged so hard on Charlie's door ten minutes ago that he wondered if someone might call the police. His heart stuttered with relief as he saw Harper in the passenger's seat.

Charlie pulled into the driveway and got out. 'Hi, Logan. I, um…just need to check on my neighbour, Eric.' He shuffled off next door, and Logan went to Harper, as she climbed from the car.

'Can we talk?' he asked, the lump in his throat so big, he could barely breathe.

'Of course.' She eyed him nervously, leading the way onto the porch, where there were two garden seats. She took one and Logan the other, although fear and urgency left him too jittery to sit still.

'Harper. I came to your apartment last night, after the gala, but obviously you weren't home.'

She shook her head. 'I couldn't face being alone with myself so I came home to Charlie.' Her eyes shone with emotion and he wished he'd dragged her into his arms the moment he'd faced her. 'Logan, I'm so sorry for last night. I should have waited to tell you about the baby. And I shouldn't have pushed you away. I just let my old insecurities, my fear of rejection, get in the way.'

'That's why I'm here, Harper,' he said, resolute, reaching for her hand. 'I'm not going to let you push me away this time. I know I failed the test when we were married. I regret that I didn't fight for us then, for you. But I won't fail you again or let you down.' He raised her hand to his lips, pressing a kiss over her knuckles. 'I love you, Harper. I always have. You are the only woman I've ever loved. I never stopped loving you in fact, not even for the ten years we were apart.'

'Logan...' she whispered, pleading, as tears spilled over her lashes.

'I want you, not just in my life, but as my life partner,' he rushed on, needing to say all the things he should have said last night. 'I want us to work together and raise our child together and grow old together. So you can push and doubt and believe that you're better off without me, but I'll never stop trying to convince you. I'll never stop loving you. I'll love you until the day I die, just like I promised when we made those marriage vows.'

She covered her mouth with her hand, crying freely now. Logan scooted closer and gripped her hand tight as if he could make her love him back. 'I know you're scared,' he whispered. 'We both are. And you were right last night. There is more at stake now, because we're going to be parents. But I'm not giving up on us, on me, you and the baby. We're a family, Harper. I'll be there for you both, every day until you believe that I won't let you down again. Until you forgive me and believe that I love you. Until you let me love you the way you deserve.'

'Logan,' she groaned, surging forward and silencing him with a kiss that was salty with her tears. 'I love you, too,' she cried. 'I believe you *now*, today, and I've already forgiven you and myself for messing up last time. I just got scared because this time, I think I love you more than before. It feels so much stronger I can hardly breathe.'

He gripped her face, his heart banging against his ribs, her amazing words turning his fear to joy. 'You do?'

She nodded, laughing through the tears still

falling. 'I want all the things you just said. I
want us to be a family, always. No giving up
on us this time. We stay together and we communicate and we work at our relationship and
we love each other hard. Because we owe it not
only to our baby but also to ourselves. We both
deserve this love.'

Because he couldn't be so far away from her,
he tugged her hand and pulled her into his lap.
He cupped her face and drew her lips to his,
kissing her the way he'd wanted to every day
since she walked back into his life. The way he
wanted to every day for the rest of their lives.

'I love you, Harper,' he said when he finally
pulled back. 'I won't let anything come between
us again, not even ourselves. It's me and you
and the baby against the world from now on,
understand?'

She gazed down at him with love, nodded
and laughed. 'Yes. Us against the world.'

Logan's heart soared, and he kissed her
again, holding her so close their hearts thudded together.

When she pulled back, he wiped the tears
from her cheeks, his own eyes burning. 'Did
you tell Charlie, about the baby?' he asked, his
excitement for fatherhood finally bubbling over
now that Harper was his again.

'Yes. Did you tell your parents?' She looked

hesitant, so he brushed her lips with his and shook his head.

'No. I was so focussed on winning you back. I did tell Sam, though. He helped me to see that I'd allowed old habits, old ways of thinking to mess with my head. And I almost lost you for a second time. I can't believe I'm that stupid.'

Harper cupped his face. 'I'm yours,' she said. 'But I don't think your parents are going to like us getting back together. They had a hard enough time with us talking last night.'

He grinned. 'Do you care? Because I don't. It's their choice if they want to be a part of their first grandchild's life or not. I told you, I only care about us.' His arms tightened around her and she breathed a kiss over his lips.

'You do know that I love you back, right?' she whispered, her feelings shining from her beautiful eyes. 'My love isn't conditional or something you have to earn. It's something that's just there, because of who you are. And it's not going anywhere. Not even I could fight it, and you know how stubborn I can be.'

Logan nodded, smiling as he captured her lips once more. 'And you do know that I'll never leave you again, right? This is it now. You're stuck with me for ever.'

Harper wrapped her arms around his neck and snuggled into his chest, sighing with what sounded like contentment. 'So where will we live? Your apartment is bigger with better views.'

'I don't care where we live,' he said, kissing the top of her head, 'as long as it's together. And first thing tomorrow, my first job as clinical lead for congenital heart surgery at Manhattan Memorial Hospital will be to offer you a permanent job.'

'You can't do that,' she said, outraged but smiling up at him. 'Employing the woman you're sleeping with is the ultimate in nepotism.'

Logan shrugged, uncaring. 'The woman I love,' he said, tilting up her chin. 'The woman I hope to one day reinstate as my wife, if she'll have me.'

Harper's stunning smile curled her mouth. 'I'm sure she will.'

'See,' he said, nuzzling the side of her neck as he breathed in her scent. 'I always win.'

EPILOGUE

'It's a girl!' Logan cried, staring down at his tiny daughter and then turning back to Harper, kissing her, brushing wisps of damp hair back from her face. 'You made us a daughter. I love you, so much.'

'I love you, too,' Harper said, both laughing and crying as she reached for their newborn, drawing her onto her chest and peering down at her with wonder that filled her heart to bursting. 'She's so beautiful.' She couldn't take her eyes off her daughter, but nor could she stop looking at Logan, who she loved a bit harder every day.

In that moment, the baby opened her eyes. She and Logan held their breath. Their daughter stared up at Harper and then closed her eyes again, instantly falling asleep.

Harper's delighted grin matched Logan's. They laughed softly together as if every move their baby made was magical and extraordinary.

'She looks just like you,' Logan said, his arm

around Harper's shoulders and his face pressed to hers as they both watched their daughter take her first nap out in the world. 'I didn't think it was possible for me to love you any more,' he whispered for Harper's ears only. 'But I do.'

She looked up at him and blinked back her tears.

'You are amazing,' he said, pressing his lips to hers once more. 'And you're going to be the best mother in the world. I just know it.'

Harper smiled, her stare torn between Logan, who wore a look of love and adoration and respect, and their miraculous baby girl. 'I think I will,' she said, feeling the certainty to the marrow of her bones. 'I'm her mother.'

'Yes, you are, my love.' He breathed into her hair, his lips pressed to her temple.

With the baby's delivery complete, their midwife carefully wrapped their precious sleeping bundle in a clean towel. 'When you're ready to take a shower, perhaps Dad could hold her. And there are three very eager grandparents outside in the waiting room.'

Logan's parents had come around to the fact they were back together, and Charlie had been their number one supporter. Harper had gone back to work part-time at MMH. She felt confident that she and Logan would find a work-life balance that suited all three of them.

'Not yet,' Harper said, still marvelling at her tiny daughter, loving their skin-to-skin contact and wondering how she would ever again put her down.

'They can wait a bit longer,' Logan added, inching onto the bed beside Harper. With one arm around Harper's shoulders and the other around the baby in her arms, the three of them formed a tight circle of love that Harper felt certain would be unbreakable.

'What shall we call her?' Harper asked, looking up at Logan to see the same wonder she was feeling on his handsome face.

'Perfection.' He said with an indulgent smile. 'Beloved. Ours,' he offered with a straight face, because of course, baby girl Grant was all of those things.

Harper nodded. 'We'll think of something. There's no rush.'

They each went back to staring at their sleeping daughter. After a few minutes, Logan said, 'Perhaps the more important question is one for you.'

'What's that?' Harper said, distracted by the length of her baby's tiny eyelashes and her miniscule finger nails. She looked up to see Logan was no longer looking at the baby, but at her, wearing the same expression of love.

'Will you marry me again, Harper?' he said,

his voice choked with emotion. 'I want us to be a family and I want *you*. Please say you'll be my wife again, because I want nothing more than to be her father.' He tilted his head in the baby's direction. 'And your husband.'

Fresh tears stung Harper's eyes. 'Yes. I will marry you again. I'm yours and you're mine.'

Logan's smile, the elation in his stare was almost as beautiful as their daughter. Almost.

'I'm going to spend the rest of my life making sure you don't regret that,' he said, kissing her with such soft tenderness, her heart almost burst with love.

'I could never regret us,' she said. 'I love you. I love our life and now I love our family.' She kissed him and smiled. 'Now who's the winner?'

They celebrated their love with another kiss.

* * * * *

Look out for the next story in the
Sexy Surgeons in the City duet
New York Nights with Mr. Right
by Tina Beckett

And if you enjoyed this story,
check out these other great reads
from JC Harroway

Forbidden Fiji Nights with Her Rival
Secretly Dating the Baby Doc
Nurse's Secret Royal Fling

All available now!

Reader Service

Enjoyed your book?

Try the perfect subscription for Romance readers and get more great books like this delivered right to your door.

See why over 10+ million readers have tried Harlequin Reader Service.

Start with a Free Welcome Collection with free books and a gift—valued over $20.

Choose any series in print or ebook. See website for details and order today:

TryReaderService.com/subscriptions